THE VOYEUR

A J. C. KAMINER MYSTERY

MICHAEL MORIARTY

SIMON & SCHUSTER

SIMON & SCHUSTER
Rockefeller Center
1230 Avenue of the Americas
New York, NY 10020

Copyright © 1997 by Michael Moriarty

Designed by Irving Perkins Associates

Manufactured in the United States of America

10 9 8 7 6 5 4 3 2 1

Library of Congress Cataloging-in-Publication Data

Moriarty, Michael, 1941–
The voyeur : a J. C. Kaminer mystery / Michael Moriarty
p.   cm.
I. Title.
PS3563.0871637V69 1997
813'.54—dc21   97-2138
CIP

ISBN 0-684-80425-5

ACKNOWLEDGMENTS

I'D LIKE TO ACKNOWLEDGE Roz Starr who introduced me to my new friend and editor, Charles Adams of Simon & Schuster, who in turn handed me over to that formidable publishing company's copyeditors, who are helping to polish this series into a winner, the fruits of which are very much in the hands of my literary agent, Nikki Smith, who in turn will continue to do with subsequent J. C. Kaminer volumes what she has already done with *The Voyeur*: nurture my work with care and, at times, infuriating reserve, but always with impeccable taste and shrewdness.

Dedicated to the great French mystery writer
Georges Simenon, and to Anne Hamilton Martin.

IN THE FALL OF 1993 I PRESENTED THIS FABLE OF MINE TO
CHARLES ADAMS OF SIMON & SCHUSTER.

ON JUNE 12, 1994, NICOLE BROWN SIMPSON WAS FOUND
STABBED TO DEATH ON THE LAWN OF HER BEVERLY HILLS HOME.

IS MY STORY PRESCIENCE AND PROPHECY? OR MERELY THE SELF-
FULFILLING VOYEURISM OF AN ENTIRE NATION?

"America, J.C., is a doin' thing."

MOTHER MAY KAMINER

PREAMBLE

Allow me to introduce myself: J. C. Kaminer. I have been variously described as a Renaissance man, a jack-of-all-trades and master of none, or a scatterbrain. You may determine for yourself which description best fits me. I personally experience states of all three and wouldn't part with one of them since each affords infinite possibilities for adventure.

*"The only people
who get anyplace interesting,"*

said Henry David Thoreau,

*"are the people
who get lost."*

And I, for one, have only the barest navigational skills, so, thus far, I may have had the most interesting life in all of New York City. On this island of lost souls, that, as is sometimes said, is sayin' something. However, to avoid any major geographic dislocation, I became a psychiatrist. This enables me to get lost in other people's lives, in the thickest undergrowth of other people's darker forests.

13

My commitment to psychiatry has been enhanced by a formidable dread of physical exertion. The sedentary posture of most psychiatrists, psychoanalysts, therapists, or any other mental racketeer also affords many blissful hours for my particular form of sexual proclivity. I am, without apology, shame, or even the slightest hint of embarrassment, a voyeur. Of all the sexual deviations, mine is the safest and, at times, the most pleasurable. I rarely suffer from the embarrassment of postcoital conversations. Some people ask, "Isn't it lonely?"

"Yes," I say, "but it's also filled with the joys of an infinite simplicity."

I attribute these tendencies to either lethargy, wisdom, or fear. Or some amusing combination of the three.

I have also, personally, undergone complete psychoanalysis, group and family therapy, the infrequent confessional of Alcoholics Anonymous, the Erhard Seminars Training, two or three mad weekends in a communal experiment, four boring months in a Zen institute, and—to make a long list incredibly shorter—any variety of overnight enlightenments offered to the American public between the years of 1963 and 1979.

Since then I have settled down to an incredibly successful confidence game of my own. I offer limitless periods of silence to anyone willing to pay me at least one hundred and fifty dollars an hour. My one remaining shred of integrity rests in the fact that I immediately increase my fees for anyone whom I consider to be malingering. It is comforting to watch people quickly confront their problems when the refusal to do so may incur immediate bankruptcy.

Now you may wonder, what is this doubtfully favorite son of Bremington, South Carolina, doing in such a Yankee enclave as New York City? Well, I personally have never considered New York City—Manhattan particularly—to be even remotely a portion of any part of the world, least of all the smugly righteous regions of North America. In fact, this nation's general desire to be rid of its biggest Babylon is the city's most outstanding recommendation. This city, my city, New York City, belongs to no particular race, no particular country—and certainly no particular set of stupid ideas. It bumbles along in the only honest way we all do: by trial and error and by confronting daily the infinite limitations afforded the human experiment. I don't know a single survivor in this metropolis who, despite the pride and arrogance of his demeanor, hasn't discovered the strangely confidence-enhancing effects of humiliation.

I

CHARLES MANES ENTERED MY OFFICE and my life with an
obligatory bend of his head. The door frame was too
short to encompass the six-seven body he gracefully
threaded through it. He walked to my desk and looked
down at me from such a towering height I was forced to
rise from my chair in simple self-defense.

After this giant, so profoundly black, so beyond purple night, had seated himself, I inquired immediately as
to his prejudices about Southern landed gentry:

"My ancestors," I began, "were slave-owners, Mr.
Manes. Do you have a problem with that?"

Charles replied that his grandfather happened to have
been hung for "slitting the throat of a Southern
landowner and raping his wife."

I don't always know whether to believe these admissions but my rule in general is to take people at face
value. It keeps me from treating the excessively sick. Not
only are they dangerous but they rarely pay their bills.

In *this* case, however, something told me the man was
lying. That "something" was the problem that had
brought him here.

17

In the previous two years, this giant had been mugged and/or robbed four times. He now traveled mostly in the company of a bodyguard.

He was also suffering similar encounters with his wife, Charlotte.

Mrs. Manes first appeared before me on January 28, 1992. In a couples therapy session with her husband who by then had been my client for three years.

She was, indeed, a very American vision.

Imperial Playboy Bunny.

A kind of royal centerfold.

Before any of us knew it she was flirting with me.

"Sullivan. Harry Stack Sullivan, correct?"

"Yes, Mrs. Manes. . . ."

"Do you call my husband Charles?"

"Yes."

"Then you can call me Charley."

I looked at her husband.

"That's her name, Dr. Kaminer. Ever since her father used to call her to dinner."

"You'll forgive me if I call you Charlotte," I said. "I hate diminutives, regardless of how charmingly they are applied."

"In that case, I won't call you Colonel Sanders."

Had Charles compared me to the Southern fried chicken king? Had they both, in their few compatible moments together, shared my silvery Southern demeanor as the butt of their humor?

18

"Mrs. Manes," I said with a smile, "I shall forever be indebted to your tact."

There was a slight pause and silence during which she seemed to relax. Her smile, which appeared genuine, seemed to say to her husband that this little meeting might be enjoyable.

"Now," I continued, "I don't wish to make this encounter the end-all and be-all of your marriage. It was my suggestion that we three meet to discover, if possible, the major, most vulnerable areas of your relationship. Those which, if you're at all interested, might save or destroy it."

"I'm sure," interrupted Mrs. Manes, "Charles has told you all about our sex life. How graphic did he get?"

I waited for her to finish.

"How explicit were the details?" She seemed to be both annoyed and interested. Her eyes flickered between anger and amused curiosity. It was hard to know which she was really faithful to. "As you might have heard from Charles, I am utterly shameless. "

I almost believed her. The clear blue of her eyes and the calm, unflinching clarity of her voice would have carried the day if the reading hadn't sounded so perfect.

She's rehearsed this, I thought. She has an agenda here that begs to be heard. Give her the rein, I thought. Let her direct things a bit.

"You don't believe me, do you?"

She was reading me as quickly as I had read her. This could be troublesome. I decided honesty might be the most surprising policy.

19

"Should I, Mrs. Manes?"

She sighed a bit at my return to formality. "Well, if you take that tone with me there's not much I can do."

"You prefer being treated as a little girl, Mrs. Manes?"

"It's always worked before," she said with a smile.

"I'm sure it has, Mrs. Manes, but since your husband has enrolled in the Kaminer Course in Obligatory Growth, your refusal to join him in the enterprise could cause considerable damage to your very precarious marriage."

"Are you gay, Dr. Kaminer?"

"Charley," interrupted her husband.

"I never know with Southern gentlemen," she continued.

"Charley," he asked, "what's that got to do with anything?"

"They're all so wordy and flowing," she said without taking her eyes off me. "It's hard to tell. I've bedded a few in my time and still don't know."

This last thought she directed at her husband. The words struck him squarely in between his good intentions and he fell quietly back into silence.

"If I hadn't heard," I offered, "that you say such things to all your men, Mrs. Manes, I'd be downright flattered."

Charlotte Manes smiled.

"We Southern gentlemen," I added, "like our counterparts in the Orient, wish to remain as inscrutable as possible."

"You still haven't answered my question," she said.

"Are you jealous, Mrs. Manes?"

"Of what?" she asked with a smile.

"All these questions about my sexuality—are you threatened in some way?"

"Should I be?" she purred.

"I certainly hope so. I'm not paid to make you feel comfortable."

"Dr. Kaminer," began her husband, "I knew Charley didn't really want—"

"Charles," she interrupted, "Dr. Kaminer can obviously take care of himself."

"Charley . . . ," he added.

"You just let us talk a bit," she said, patting him on the hand. "I'm the one in trouble here."

She paused and then looked at me.

"Isn't that true, Doctor? Aren't I the problem child?"

"Charles is my patient, Mrs. Manes," I said. "His marriage is the only problem child I'm concerned with right now."

Mrs. Manes then asked with venomous insincerity: "You think there's some hope for us?"

Her head began bobbing with a Barbie Doll expression.

"Charley," groaned her husband.

"Shut up!" she said. "You asked me to come here. Begged me, and what did I say?"

Charles Manes waited for her to continue.

"I said, 'Fine!' Didn't I? 'Fine!'"

This last word was thrown at him.

"As long," she continued, "as I can say what I damn well please!"

By now Charles Manes was nodding in defeated agreement with everything she said.

21

"Did you think I was just jerking off?!"

Charles looked across the desk at me in crucified silence.

"I don't jerk off, Charles! I fuck! I fuck you! I fuck him!" she said, pointing in my direction. "Whether he likes it or not," she proclaimed with amazingly controlled abandon, "I put it out there! And they all go limp. That's the way it is with the truth! It sets you free and it scares the hell out of everybody else!"

After the painful silence that ensued, I asked: "Do you care at all about this marriage, Mrs. Manes?"

After a slight pause for thought, she looked over at her husband, studied his face for a while, and then said: "I don't know, Doctor. But it's not my marriage I'm here for."

After a pause, she continued: "I'm looking for some help of my own. I'm shopping for an adviser. You sounded amusing."

"Charles," I said, "would you excuse us for a minute?"

Charlotte's husband rose to his full and incredibly naive-looking height. He looked at his wife and said: "Charley, please don't take it out on Dr. Kaminer."

"Leave, Charles," she ordered.

He sat down again and leaned toward her.

"Charley, I'll leave when you tell me you're sorry for insulting me."

"Insulting you?!" she gasped in mock hilarity.

"Yes, Charley," he said, grabbing her hands gently but firmly.

"Let go of my hands," she murmured in a low but angry tone.

"Why?" he asked. "Am I hurting you?"

"No." She looked away. "But you might."

"Have I ever hurt you, Charley?" he asked.

She didn't answer.

"Charley?"

"What?" she mumbled.

"Have I ever physically hurt you in any way?"

"You poor sap," she said, looking at her husband. "You don't get it, do you?"

She looked over at me. "Maybe I like a little pain." She paused. "Have you thought of that?"

Charles Manes let go of his wife's hands.

"He's a really nice guy, Doc," she went on. "No drugs . . . oh, a little pot a few years back, but the poor puppy couldn't stay happy. Went on a bummer, didn't you, baby? And he never did it again. There are a lot of things he doesn't ever want to do again. Isn't that true, sweetface?"

This last she said with affection. She touched his face quite gently. Then kissed him on the eyes. "Christ just wouldn't approve, would he, baby?"

"Will you apologize, Charley?"

"For what, sweetface?"

"For hurting me," he said simply. "For treating me like an idiot."

After a small but highly evasive move of the head, she said, "Sort of."

23

Charles looked at her in silence.

"I sort of apologize."

She then waited.

Charles said nothing.

"Isn't that good enough?"

Again another pause.

"I'm sort of sorry!" she repeated.

Charles rose and left the room.

Within seconds Mrs. Manes was crying. I pulled my box of Kleenex from the drawer. She pulled her own handkerchief from her pocketbook. It was a studiously old-fashioned thing with lightly crocheted borders. A luxurious item for such a necessary task.

"I can't advise you, Mrs. Manes."

"I know that," she said quickly. "I know that much about therapy and ethics. I thought you might know of someone."

I did, ironically. This physician's name had come to mind almost immediately. The second she had tried to flirt with me.

"Yes, Mrs. Manes. Yes, I do know of someone. A Dr. Brockman. A Dr. Marion Brockman."

"A woman?"

She looked almost fearful.

"Yes. I think she's exactly what you're looking for."

"I wasn't looking for a woman."

"But that's what you need, Mrs. Manes. A male therapist would only further complicate your already confounding situation."

"Has Charles spoken a lot about me?"

24

"Enough for me to know that you are in considerably greater pain than he."

She wasn't the least surprised or defensive at my analysis.

"Did he say I was a nymphomaniac?".

Here her nervous head moves gave away an almost bottomless reservoir of guilt.

"He mentioned that others had said so."

"How kind of him. Or you. To lie for him."

I refused to take the bait. The tears began again. Her handkerchief by now was small and wet and rolled into a little ball.

"I shouldn't let you seduce me, should I? I mean your manner shouldn't make me trust you too much."

"That's a very good beginning, Mrs. Manes. I think Dr. Brockman will prove immensely helpful to you in that respect."

"As you might expect," she said simply, "I don't get along with women very well."

"Well, 'getting along' with your therapist is not the object of the enterprise."

"What is, Doctor?"

"The truth."

She looked across the desk at me.

"The very thing you said everyone's so afraid of."

She nodded in a slightly sarcastic manner. "So I'm frightened of the truth, am I?"

"I didn't say that, did I?"

"No, but that's what you meant."

"Mrs. Manes, I'm not here to convince you of my sin-

25

cerity. Since I can't accept you as a client there's no necessity of my doing so."

At this, she nodded in simple agreement.

"However," I continued, "your instant distrust of everything I say is a clear indication of how much pain you are in. Charles has been with me for three years. I pride myself not only on the increased strength of his performance on the basketball court but on his behavior and increased self-esteem generally."

I waited for her to rebut my offering.

She remained silent.

"At this point, only the chaos of your marriage appears to be insurmountable."

Her head circled in little pouting turns. "So I'm the problem?"

I waited.

"I'm the only thing in the way?"

"In the way of what, Mrs. Manes?"

"Of Charles becoming Michael Jordan?"

"Nothing," I said most emphatically, "not you, nor I, nor the happiest marriage imaginable, can imbue within Charles Manes the genius of Michael Jordan!"

My forceful delivery seemed to delight Mrs. Manes. I wished I hadn't been quite so entertaining. Sexual messages were reappearing.

"That is something," I pressed on, "Charles himself is coming to terms with."

I sat back in my chair. My added remarks were now addressed as much to myself as to Mrs. Manes: "The growing realization of his limitations, ironically, has improved his game."

"Well, you're quite the little miracle worker, aren't you!"

Evidently my withdrawal from the sexual battlefield had angered her.

"Marion Brockman," I continued after a slight sigh at her sarcasm, "is my best recommendation. Take it or leave it."

She paused, knotted the handkerchief in her hand even more tightly, looked about herself in aimless frustration, and then said: "I'll take it."

II

"Marion?"

"Yes, J.C.?"

"I have referred someone to you."

"I know, she's already called. We have an appointment this coming Monday."

"I don't want to influence your diagnosis. I know how irritating that can be."

"Yes."

"While I realize that it has been some time since we last spoke, I do hope we may talk. My concern, of course, is less with the woman I have sent you than with her husband, and I trust that you will be able to shed some light on what is going on between them once you have come to know Mrs. Manes."

Marion's silence on the other end of the line was deafening.

"May I call you?"

After the slightest pause, she replied: "Anytime."

Chances are that no one overhearing this exchange would ever guess that for a period of time, albeit brief, Dr. Brockman and I had "put the plum in the golden vase," to paraphrase the ancient Chinese author Chin P'ing Mei. No one except Dr. Brockman, that is. Her ear for the subtext of a voice, any voice—including her own—is unerring. Were she to overhear this brief exchange she might quickly observe: "Those two people have shared more than diagnoses."

III

"I LOVE HER," SAID CHARLES MANES. "I can't help it. No matter what she does, I can't leave."

He waited for me to say something.

I didn't.

He looked up at me.

"When she's sincere," he continued, "when she touches my cheek and calls me 'sweetface,' that's when I know she loves me, too."

He paused.

"I still know," he continued, "I'm the best man she's ever been with."

"How do you mean, Charles?" I asked.

He looked up at me.

"I don't understand," I added. "What do you mean by 'the best man'?"

"Goodness. Just plain goodness. I'm a good man."

Again he waited for me to say something.

Again I refused.

"I've never hit her," he went on. "I've never humiliated her no matter what she did to me. I always held her gently. I know she's tried to make me angry, but I just won't do it."

"Why not, Charles?" I asked.

He looked up.

"What's wrong with your anger?"

"Anger?" he replied, with a look of slightly shocked surprise. "It's terrible. It's the worst. Have you ever seen me angry in here?"

"No, Charles," I said. "Are you afraid of showing it?"

"What?"

"What's wrong with anger?"

He looked at me as if I'd asked him what was wrong with homicide.

"Well, you've obviously never seen me angry."

"No, Charles, I haven't."

"It's pretty frightening."

His head bobbed and weaved in a little dance of memory.

"For whom, Charles? Who's it most frightening to?"

"Anybody," he said quickly. "I've scared anybody I was around with my anger."

"You didn't scare those muggers," I said.

He looked at me for a moment.

"I never got angry," he said. "It all happened so fast."

"Anger's pretty fast," I offered. "It's usually up and over before you know it."

"I know," he said. "That's why I watch it. I watch it like a hawk."

A silence fell between us.

He looked out the window briefly, then turned toward me.

He paused.

"Is that bad?" he asked.

"Is what bad?" I asked.

"To feel anger," he said, and then added, "or to feel so bad about anger that you can't get angry?"

I waited.

"Is that what I'm doing? Being too frightened of my anger?"

I continued to wait. I certainly didn't want to interrupt this line of thought.

"I remember my mama."

"Yes?" I replied.

"I was fifteen and already pretty big then and I busted her dinnerware."

He looked at me for a response.

"I just tossed it all around the kitchen because she told me I couldn't spend the night at Larry Hanes' house. He had a pretty bad rep and she knew it."

He paused in the middle of his own memories.

"She didn't talk to me for a month."

He looked up at me.

"For four weeks my mama refused to even say hello."

He looked down at the floor.

"There'd be breakfast in the morning on the table . . . dinner set for one at night . . . she wouldn't spend more than three seconds in the same room with me. I had to sit in that house all by myself."

At this point Charles' voice began to fill with tears.

"I never felt so bad in my whole life. I'd cry myself to sleep and it still didn't make any difference to her."

He lifted his right hand to wipe away the tears.

"Finally, one month to the second almost, she said: 'Charles? I don't want you ever, ever, ever, ever, ever'— oh, she must have said it ten times . . . 'ever, ever, ever to be angry in front of me again!'"

He looked up at me.

"'Not even a scowl!' she said."

Charles' head nodded repeatedly in the memory.

"And I never did," he said. "To the day she died, I never again showed her one ounce of anger."

A long pause ensued during which I wondered which had been worse for Charles Manes: the month of silence or these years of shame.

"You were angry again, though," I said. "Didn't your mama still make you angry?"

"Yeah," he said with a slight pause, "but each time I walked right out of the house. I went out on the street and I took a lot of deep breaths and walked around the block if I had to, but I wouldn't show her an angry face."

"Is that what you do with Charlotte?" I asked.

He nodded his head.

"Does it go away?"

He looked up at me.

"Does the anger leave you?"

"Sometimes," he mumbled.

"What do you do when it doesn't?"

"I think of what my mama did to me and I cry."

He said this and then nodded yes, as if the gesture would make things clearer for him.

"And then it goes away," he said. "Yup, I think about all the pain I suffered for being angry and I cry and I'm just not angry anymore."

He said this with such pride it almost broke my heart.

IV

"DR. KAMINER?" CHARLOTTE MANES' VOICE caressed my ears with surprising grace and simplicity.

I had been looking out the window of my office. I turned to see her standing politely in the doorway, awaiting my reply.

"Mrs. Manes," I said with some nervous expectation.

"I didn't want to call you on the phone because, well, I just didn't want to use the phone. I'm here to thank you in person."

I waited.

"May I come in?"

"Yes," I said with only mild reluctance.

She entered the room and sat on my couch.

"Dr. Brockman is wonderful."

"Oh," I said with some relief. "Yes, yes, well, so things are working out for you?"

"Yes, yes they are."

There was an awkward pause.

"I'm not sure," she continued, "if it will save my marriage, but it has done a great deal of good for my self-respect."

She smiled.

"It's nice to know," she said, "that a woman can be free without being cruel about it."

She looked to me for a response.

"I apologize," she continued, "for my rudeness during our last encounter."

I would have liked to comfort her with some passing dismissal of the memory, but my professional guard had gone up like a duck blind.

"I just wanted you to know, Dr. Kaminer, that I love my husband. Whatever impression I may have made before, all my glibness about Charles and our marriage, well, it's not how I really feel for most of the time."

Her visit had, of course, inspired a million questions in me, but I was not about to entertain them for long. It was barely a month since I'd seen her and though improvements can be made in therapy, miracles are to be profoundly distrusted. This new and improved Charlotte Manes would best be helped by continued suspicion.

As if on cue, she said: "I know you still don't trust me, but, well, it doesn't matter. I'm doing this for me and I feel a lot better for having seen you in person."

At that point she rose and extended her right hand politely. "Goodbye, Dr. Kaminer."

Startled at the abruptness of her departure, I smiled nervously and returned the favor. Placing my hand in hers, I said: "Goodbye, Mrs. Manes."

She turned toward the door.

"And continued good fortune," I added.

She paused just briefly without turning, and then left the room.

V

I FIRST HEARD OF CHARLOTTE MANES' untimely death in the august pages of the International *Herald-Tribune*. On the twenty-first of August, to be precise. I was lying on the beach and in the earliest stages of my yearly flirtation with skin cancer.

Her death was described as a murder. Five stab wounds. One to the belly, another to the shoulder, a third through the neck, and one through the back that had apparently reached her heart. A final slash had been laid across the throat. Not a shy assailant.

There was no mention of her husband as a possible killer.

On the day of my flight home, however, greeting me garishly from the Kennedy Airport newsstands was the cover of this city's boldest tabloid, a publication I read religiously for the sole purpose of entertainment—as I said, I am a voyeur, and, therefore, the *New York Post* is an integral part of my deviation. There on the front page was a photo of my client, his head held as nobly as possible under the circumstance of being led out of the Midtown South precinct house. Over the photo was emblazoned the words:

Was Wizard The One?

"Wizard" was Charles Manes' game name, the invariable encomium laid upon anyone averaging over twenty-five points a game—Wizard, Magic, Doctor—all with just a hint of voodoo, if you ask me.

Was Wizard the one?

I didn't know. I honestly had no idea whether he had stabbed his wife or not, as I would later tell him.

Was I personally pained at the news of her death?

Yes.

Did I collect my personal impressions of her and confess to myself that she had, perhaps, cut through my "professionalism"?

Yes.

And, yes, I did reconsider our brief history together.

And, with a final yes, I had desired her.

I had also made occasionally callous jokes about her.

These cruelties are common when terminal patients begin to cut through a physician's armor. In my case I had had no way of knowing Charlotte Manes was terminal. I had only seen her twice, but I think I must have heard her name repeated in the secrecy of my office at least a thousand times before she died.

"Charles," I said at our session following Labor Day on Wednesday, September 9, 1993, "before we begin this session it would be unfair of me either to feign ignorance of your predicament or to blithely exonerate you of something I'm so unsure of. I have to ask you point-blank: Did you kill your wife?"

"No."

He said this simply and with such pained resignation that I almost accepted it.

"In all honesty," I added after a silence very uncomfortable for both of us, "I can picture you in some dreadful set of circumstances losing your control."

He nodded.

"I don't particularly want to talk about it," he said, "but I also can't see avoiding the truth. I'm back in it again. I've kind of mugged myself here, haven't I?"

"Perhaps."

I wasn't about to exclude the possibility that his marriage had been a mugging from the outset and that his present bereavement, incriminating as it was, held some promise in it. Perhaps even a sign of cure.

"Do you have any idea who might have done it?"

Charles looked at me with a slight hint of dismay. "Doctor, I'm more interested in how I feel right now than who did it."

"Charles, if we find out who really did it, I guarantee you it will instantly improve how you feel now. We have increased your shooting average and I am determined not to see that achievement go to waste on the courts of Ossining Penitentiary."

At last he smiled and nodded in agreement.

"Who, aside from you, would want to murder your wife?"

"Shouldn't we leave this to my lawyer?"

"No. That dreadful man called me and suggested I help you plead temporary insanity. He has gone, as you so vividly describe it, 'belly up.'"

Charles looked at me almost coyly.

"You don't think that's a good idea?"

"Charles, I'm beginning to believe you did it."

A rather disturbing little smile crept upon his lips.

"I would have liked to," he said finally.

He waited to see the effect of his words on me. I, of course, remained my brilliantly inscrutable self.

"I honestly dreamed of putting more than a knife into her."

"What exactly do you mean by that?" I asked.

"She was a nymphomaniac, Doctor. There wasn't anything I could do to satisfy her. She demanded so much that I began to hope she'd die in the act, you know."

He took a deep breath. The anger was just beginning to surface.

"I thought maybe if I brought the local football team over!"

He held this sentence in midair.

"I thought they might finally put her out of her misery!"

I remembered that she had referred to herself as a "nymphomaniac" during the first of our two meetings. Charles had, of course, previously described some of Charlotte's proclivities. He had also discussed his feelings of inadequacy, and Charlotte's behavior in our one couple therapy session had corroborated much of this.

"Yeah, I wanted her dead. Someone did me a favor."

"Then tell me how you did it. Tell me how you killed her."

Charles looked at me and scoffed like a child. His head moved uncomfortably from side to side.

"You hired someone? To do you a favor," I added, hoping the remark might provoke him in some direction, any direction but the one he seemed mired in.

He wouldn't answer.

The most moving and bizarre part of my profession is the occasional vision of creatures like Charles Manes, all six foot seven inches of him, looking like babes in diapers.

"Christ said," he murmured finally, "if you even feel hate, you're guilty."

"I beg your pardon," I offered sincerely.

"My mama told me about my feelings. Said to watch 'em. Watch 'em like a hawk. Then bring 'em to Christ. That if I didn't pray for help with my anger, it would just take me over."

"Yes?"

"Wasn't enough, I guess."

"What wasn't enough, Charles?"

He shifted uneasily and then said, "Prayin'. My prayers."

"I guess. Isn't that why you're here with me?"

"Yeah, and it's probably why I'll go to jail."

Tears began to form in his eyes.

"You're scared, huh?"

"Yeah. Never been so scared."

He began to cry. Quite audibly. I'm grateful my office is at the back of my apartment. My waiting patients can't really hear much below a shout. He seemed to know that and began to let it all out, trying to cover his face with his hands, bowing his head and letting all those tears drop right on the edge of my oriental rug. There aren't many such intimacies blessing it. Most of my crying patients

41

come prepared. Women particularly. Some have asked
for a Kleenex and I proffer them one from my drawer. I
hesitate to leave the box out for display. It seems manipulative to me.

In this instance, however, I took the box out and
pushed it across the desk toward Charles.

"I didn't do it," he mumbled.

I waited.

"I know it doesn't look that way, but I didn't do it, and
I didn't hire anyone else to do it. At least, I don't think I
did."

It was at this point that I first began to believe him.

"Am I being led to understand that you somehow, at
some time, somewhere, suggested the possibility that
your wife's demise might please you considerably, might
encourage you to be incredibly grateful in one way or another?"

"Dooby," he said.

"Dooby?"

"He's my driver. I really couldn't keep it a secret from
him. I mean he's heard so many of our arguments."

"He's your driver?"

"And my bodyguard," said Charles with a slight hint
of embarrassment. "He carries a gun."

"Oh?" I questioned.

"He's licensed for a weapon."

"I would certainly hope so," I added quickly.

"I didn't want to buy a pistol," he continued, "because
I honestly thought I might use it."

"On your wife."

He paused, thought a bit, and then said, with sad resignation: "Yes."

"But, Charles, whom do you expect your bodyguard to use it on?"

"The Mob."

I suddenly began to feel very uncomfortable. I had the instant, paranoid vision of a speeding car crammed with armed gangsters somehow levitating to my third floor and pumping a full load of blazing missiles into my charming little office. There are many prized possessions adorning the walls and side tables. All of my numerous diplomas and honorary degrees (in many diverse fields, I might add—Doctor of Music, Doctor of Fine Arts, two from the University of Rome), not to mention the many novels and plays adorning the bookshelves that house not only the complete works of Freud and Jung in their first leather-bound editions, but also James Joyce, William Shakespeare, the Jerusalem Bible, and the complete letters of Vincent van Gogh. Yes, into the vulnerably protective armor of glass and leather the bullets would scream, piercing all that might basically encompass the intellectual history of Western Civilization, virtually annihilating whatever margin of transcendence I might have attained in my over twenty-five years of practice. I felt strangely exposed and excited.

"Charles," I inquired, "are you referring to the Cosa Nostra?"

"Yeah, the Mafia. They tried to get me to fix a few games and I wouldn't do it."

"They asked you to lose games?"

"No, shave points. They set a point spread. . . ."

I gave Charles my most theatrically bewildered expression.

"If we're to win, the bet is usually by how much. How many points. They approached me and told me the spread. I told them to take a hike but the spread came out that way anyway. I found an envelope with fifteen thousand dollars sitting in my locker. I knew they'd be back, so I waited and when they asked again I handed them back their money. They videotaped the meeting so it looks like some kinda deal anyway, tried to blackmail me, and I told them if any of them ever approach me again I'll go to the police."

"Did they believe you?"

"Well, they haven't come back, but if they do, it won't be to bargain."

"They wouldn't kill a famous basketball player. Doesn't make sense. Could only hurt them. They kill each other, don't they? I mean, isn't that how it works in that fraternity? Isn't that what they plan in their little social clubs?"

Charles did not respond.

"I'm not saying you're entirely paranoid, but I hardly think a gun is necessary."

"Doctor?"

"Yes?"

"I don't plan to have my arms broken or all of my teeth knocked out. They may not kill me, but they *do* do those things."

"I see."

We sat in silence for quite some time. The predicament, the dual predicament Mr. Manes found himself in, was quite conducive to speechlessness. I was mildly dumbstruck by the dilemma. Beyond the rock and the hard place, Mr. Manes also found himself sitting in the fat, simmering in the grease of his wife's apparently terminal infidelities.

"Charles, I am becoming not a little upset with you. It is not my job to enforce honesty, to demand full disclosure. However, like your lawyer, I cannot proceed without some sense of candidness. You have for the past three and a half years regaled me with your sexual exploits and the unfortunate habit your wife has of belittling them. At no time did you mention even the slightest run-in with blackmail attempts or Italian hooligans."

After a suitably humiliated pause, Charles chose to change the subject with, "You don't like my lawyer, do you?"

"I don't believe I said that. I do believe I evinced a thorough distaste for his incipient plea. I do not consider now, then, or at any time in the foreseeable future your being able to plead insanity, temporary or otherwise— not with my understanding of you. Not with the commitment you made to ending your victimization. There is no more penultimate victim than the suspect, guilty or not, who pleads insanity."

Again the Manes silence. There wasn't much time left to our session.

"What would I have to do," he murmured, "to prove to you that I was insane?"

45

"This may come as a major surprise to you, Mr. Manes, but I do not believe in insanity."

How might I describe Mr. Manes' reaction? His eyes didn't so much widen as retreat. There was a looking within so immediate, so filled with did-I-hear-what-I-thought-I-heard, that I wasn't sure he understood.

"Charles? Aside from the strength of all self-fulfilling fantasies, and I emphasize *fantasies,* insanity is a lie established by a liberal community to gain power under the guise of benevolence. And after thirty years' firsthand experience with mental institutions, I find them, for the most part, at least ten rungs on the moral ladder below prisons. Hypocrisy, as your mama's friend Mr. Jesus believed, is, was, and always will be our fiercest opponent. So don't raise the specter of insanity with me. I will terminate treatment immediately and, if you will it, prescribe the most agonizing and harshly instructive set of electroshock treatments I can devise to instruct you in the comparative experiences between commitment and incarceration. If you care to be a victim, I will most gladly oblige at being your victimizer."

Mr. Manes looked suitably clarified.

"Do I scare you?"

"Yes," he nodded.

"Good."

"Now I don't know where I am."

"At the end of your hour."

VI

CHARLES MANES, DESPITE HIS FORMIDABLE HEIGHT, was, until he began therapy, considered only average in the world of basketball. As a guard, though apparently not of the play-making variety, he filled his role admirably but without distinction. None of the recent tributes given the likes of Reggie Miller of the Pacers had come to him until he began his impressively diligent exercise in self-discovery.

Though not quite as winning, Charles' smile had a touch of Magic Johnson to it. Even with my justifiable pride in withholding almost all of my true feelings from a patient, Mr. Manes could wend his way past my wary gaze and into what is, admittedly, a vast reservoir of sentiment within me. If betrayed, however, these softer feelings can quickly congeal to hatred. That is why I guard them with such ferocity. I certainly have no wish to make an enemy of my patients and therefore I never, and I mean never, let them beyond the impenetrable walls of my fortress.

In Charles' case, however, his smile could not help but bring a wave of childlike reverie upon me. I recall envisioning an early play-companion of my youth, Willy Mavis, the son of my mother's maid, a toddling child with an infectious smile and giggle. Past the age of eight he was not allowed in the house again. Apparently his mother had caught him stealing and refused to risk her job because of the frailties of her son.

Now, decades later and aeons removed, I watched my patient sporadically smile his way through hours of confession and felt at times incapable of seeing him objectively. Only willfulness on my part, our obvious age difference, and the very foreign and very Northern tones of his voice kept me from lapsing into nostalgia.

Charles' childhood had been spent on a farm near Dearborn, Michigan. A single hoop that hung from his mother's garage saved him from national obscurity.

"'Charles,' my mama would cry, 'when you gonna realize that life ain't basketball?'"

Charles mumbled this with one of his shy smiles and instant visions of Willy Mavis crept over me.

"'Comin', Mama,' I'd say and stay out there another hour shootin' hoops."

Charles' mother had died in the early eighties, a few years before we met. I asked him if he'd felt more exposed because of that death. More vulnerable.

"Hadn't really thought about it. Maybe. Yeah, maybe."

"You miss your mama?" I asked.

"Yup."

"What did she think of Charlotte?"

Charles just looked at me, his head rocking in small, doubting bobs.

Then he said, "She did her best. They both did. Charlotte laughing and kissing and hugging and my mama smiling, but you could see the problem. Charlotte scared Mama."

"She scared everyone, didn't she?" I asked.

"Yup. Pretty much."

VII

"YOU ARE AN ACQUIRED TASTE, J.C.," said Mother May.

"What do you mean by that?" I asked.

"Your use of words like *'badinage'* and modifying phrases like 'tenderly pitying.' They put most people— certainly most Americans—off."

"Well, that most assuredly is not my intent," I replied, showing only a modicum of the irritation I felt. "Besides, Mother, these are all words I learned while worshiping at your feet."

"When," she asked, "have I ever used the word *'badinage'*?"

"Mother May," I hastened to say in my most coldly formal tones, "of all the flowery passages I have ever heard, let alone spoken, none have surpassed your own displays, your own ineluctable penchant for purple pensivities, for the indulgent ecstasies of an arboreal elaboration!"

"Your uncle Henry, J.C.," countered Mother May just as fiercely. "He outdid the Bible itself. And like some of the finer but more dangerous things in life, you and your uncle Henry A. and, now that I think of it, the Good Book itself have made almost as many enemies as friends."

50

Mother was looking at me over her half-glasses as she watered the Indian pipes, flowers she'd loved since the Emily Dickinson first edition. Grampa Kaminer had read to her from that Mabel Loomis Todd compilation and Mother remembers staring at the cover. On it the Todd drawing of Indian pipes intrigued her. She had confessed quite brazenly one night that it was their phallic quality that obsessed her. It was that memory I recalled as Mother escorted me into her dining room to attend to our ritual afternoon tea.

"A nymphomaniac?!" hummed Mother as she sat before the beautifully appointed table.

Persephone's eyes widened as she placed the sandwich tidbits and pastry desserts on the table.

"Possibly, Mother."

"Thank you, Persephone," said Mother pointedly.

The family maid for almost fifty years quickly left the room.

"At what point, J.C., does a woman stop being a sexual partner and begin transforming herself into a nymphomaniac?"

After giving Mother the lidded expression I had learned from sitting at her knee, the one she usually reserved for relatives, I said: "Multiple partners, Mother. Indiscriminate sexual contact with a variety of acquaintances and strangers."

"So what is just sowing one's oats for a young man is nyphomanicizing for women?"

"Not anymore, Mother," I droned as the crisis over which crustless tea snack I was drawn to lengthened.

51

"Acquired Immune Deficiency Syndrome has taken care of all of that. Now many of us sit around and masturbate."

While selecting the turkey with mayonnaise, I looked at Mother to see how she had taken that remark. Her mouth was full to bursting with a prune Danish, the delight she'd grown addicted to while living in Manhattan. It was my privileged duty to see her supplied with same on my monthly visits from the city to her home in Bremington.

"Masturbate either separately," I added, "or together."

"Is that what you and Marion do now?" she asked primly as she wiped the corner of her mouth with one of the exquisitely laundered, lace-edged linen napkins Persephone had set for us.

Again my lidded sigh.

"Marion and I have not exchanged so much as an innuendo for five years, Mother."

"I thought you said you were seeing her on Monday."

"I am."

Mother stopped to watch me jaw nervously on my sandwich bits.

"How do you feel about that?"

By now her hands were clasped gently before her chin, her elbows resting on the table, and the smile on her lips had reached her eyes.

"Frankly, Mother, I'm terrified."

Mother waited.

"I'm not sure what I'll say. Or do," I confessed.

Mother continued to wait.

"So I scheduled our meeting at an entirely neutral venue."

Mother's eyes just kept picking away at my defenses in much the same way as I was sucking turkey from between my teeth.

"The Palm Court of the Plaza Hotel."

Mother's expression did not change. I was determined, however, not to venture further in this direction until I'd heard from Her Royal Highness.

"The Plaza Hotel, J.C., is about as neutral for you as a brothel."

"It's not the hotel I was interested in, Mother. It's the exposed nature of the Palm Court. No possible assignation could begin in its train station ambiance. Not only are you subject to the gazes of fellow luncheoners, but disinterested strangers, fat-pocketed tourists from Hawaii, can ogle and gaze at the goin's-on."

"You're there to discuss business."

"Charlotte Manes, to be exact."

"The dead nymphomaniac."

"Precisely."

"Then you should have no trouble whatsoever, J.C. Discussing nymphomania with Marion Brockman in the Palm Court of your favorite hideaway should prove utterly dry and technical."

VIII

"Dr. kaminer?"

"Yes?"

"This is Harold Meyer, I'm. . . ."

"You are Mr. Manes' attorney and I have avoided calling you as long as possible. I have read your letter to me, and this plea strategy of yours is deplorable, I can't abide by it, I won't—"

"Dr. Kaminer, please, just hold on a minute."

"No, you hold on, sir, I have no intention of participating in your charade."

"Not guilty! Doctor? We are pleading not guilty. Does that satisfy you?"

After a pause, I replied: "Is it true? Are you certain Charles didn't do it?"

After another pause at the end of his line, I heard: "No, but does that matter?"

"Not to me, Mr. Meyer. I hope you get him off. The whole thing could very well be justifiable homicide. I am worried about Charles. Does he think he's guilty? What idea of himself is he carrying around?"

"Well, that's not my concern. I was just wondering if you would agree to testify about some particulars."

"I doubt it."

"His wife. I understand you had a couple therapy session with his wife."

"I did, and referred her immediately to Dr. Marion Brockman. You may call her if you wish."

"I have, and she wasn't very helpful."

"It's a difficult matter, Mr. Meyer. Doctor/patient privilege is just that. A privilege. And therefore a responsibility. It is not to be bandied about."

"She's dead, Dr. Kaminer."

"Precisely. And her reputation, for better or for worse, is as *she* left it. And nothing in her arrangement with either myself or Dr. Brockman included the smallest addition to or subtraction from the memory of Mrs. Charlotte Manes as she left it."

"That gallantry, Dr. Kaminer, may cost you your client's life."

IX

THE SIGN READ:

STILLMAN, MARKELY, BARKELY,
BERESFORD, SIMON
AND
MEYER

"Mr. Meyer will see you now, Doctor."

The secretary pointed to a door to the right of her desk. I entered, abandoning all good intentions.

"Thank you, Doctor, for coming. It makes things a lot easier."

While still standing, I stated my conditions: "I have an appointment in precisely forty-five minutes at a location which is minimally ten minutes from here. That gives us precisely one half hour."

"Please be seated."

I took the chair furthest from his desk, so he could either speak to me coldly from a distance, which I would have preferred, or creep toward me with unctuously ingratiating smiles. Unfortunately, he chose the latter, slithering around the back of his desk with all the ingratiating oil at his disposal to a coy little perch at the front.

"Mrs. Manes' family would like to prosecute in Connecticut."

"Yes?"

"It's entirely possible the murder occurred there."

"So."

"If Charles is convicted of the murder in Connecticut, he could be executed."

"Hmmmmm," I heard myself saying as I leaned back in my chair.

"Hmmmm," I heard again as I realized the full extent of Charles' predicament.

"Yes, Doctor. 'Hmmmm,' indeed."

Mr. Meyer's office was on the twenty-fifth floor of a Sixth Avenue skyscraper. His view of mid-Manhattan was formidable. The Citicorp Building rose to his right, the 666 Building to his left, the park stretched to the north with such an inviting array of fall colors that I almost lost my train of thought.

"If the case is tried in New York," continued Mr. Meyer, "I assure you that we will plead not guilty. If, however, it is moved to Connecticut, I have no alternative but to try and save his life the only way I know how."

"What determines the trial venue?"

"A reevaluation of the time of death and the evidence of a supposedly forthcoming witness."

"A witness?"

"Someone who placed Mrs. Manes within Connecticut state lines near the time of her death."

"Who is this person?"

"That's just it. The Manes' attorney is not obliged to convince me of anything. This decision is solely the concern of the Manhattan D.A. Only he can stop extradition."

"But hasn't Charles an alibi that puts him in New York at this juncture?"

"No."

"Where was he all this time?"

"In his car."

I waited for Mr. Meyer to elaborate.

"With no destination in mind—he says the car is where he does his best thinking."

"He has," I offered, "entrusted a similar claim to me, so it is entirely possible that is where he really was. However, I can imagine how difficult it might be to corroborate that with any witness."

"Oh, there was a witness."

"Yes?"

"Unfortunately, she is dead."

"You do know," I offered, after recognizing the judiciously theatrical style of Mr. Meyer's presentation, "that the citizens of New York are just itching to enact the death penalty and our efforts to save Charles from Connecticut law may very well end with his deeper, darker, and more ruthlessly impatient fall into a new and improved Manhattan penal code."

"I'm not a prophet, Dr. Kaminer," he offered politely. "I can only defend my client from existing legislation. Ask me to read the future and you expect of me something even Christ could not have asked for."

He paused here to allow me the time to respond. I was by that time utterly silenced eloquence. Completely persuaded by his erudition.

"As you know," he continued, "no one, not even yourself, hated lawyers more than Jesus of Nazareth."

X

MARION BROCKMAN HAS THE DISARMING élan of an extremely aggressive gazelle. From somewhere within her doe brown eyes and almost fragile features there arises a very pantherlike confidence which quickly invades one's own insecurities with her distinctive brand of privileged certainty. All the best schools, all the best admirers and all the best enemies. It is rumored that Patrick Buchanan and Elliott Abrams, two of life's least deserving intelligences, were driven upon their first encounter with her to excuse themselves lest they lay hands on a woman. Among her colleagues she has been attacked as a clone of Dr. Thomas Szasz. His distrust of our profession dwarfs my own, and the violence of her essays on the subject even frightens me at times. The sight of her waiting for me in the Palm Court of the Plaza Hotel was mystically imposing, her head held at an angle that conveyed the knowledge of other worlds, a communion with darker smiles and brighter destinies.

"Marion," I said gently as I approached.

She looked up and smiled her disturbingly peaceful smile.

"I'm not late, am I?"

"I don't know. Are you?"

I was about to consult my pocket watch when I realized she was being coy. Holding me to earlier promises. Evoking in me the pain of older secrets.

"Marion," I said more intensely than I wished to, "when are you going to forgive me?"

"For what?" She sat there and waited for me to call up sins which perhaps even she hadn't considered.

"For not living up to your expectations."

That felt good. It seemed to cover the problem without giving anything away.

She looked at me coldly and then placed her half-glasses on her nose to consult the menu. "I'm starved and you can afford the most expensive things on the menu."

"Yes, I can," I said proudly, "and I can't think of anyone I'd rather feed them to than you."

After a lightly withering glance, she went back to inspecting the menu. By now the waiter had arrived.

"The steak, please."

"Yes, madam."

"Rare."

"And for you, sir?"

"A tuna salad sandwich, please."

"Anything to drink?"

"Wine."

"Water."

We replied simultaneously but by then the waiter had no problem distinguishing tastes.

"Red, madam?"

"Yes, please."

Yes, Marion and I had had a "thing" at one time. It was brief but very intense. Within a few days we had offered up to each other not only our bodies and our minds, but our entire psychic privacy as well. A rendezvous lasting fifty-two hours with no sleep, no inhibitions, and not one ounce of common sense. Of course, an equally ludicrous argument ensued, and after a cooling-off period of about five years we had reached a congenial distrust of not only each other but, when in each other's company, ourselves as well.

"The Manes couple," I offered, hoping to get the meeting off to a businesslike start.

"The late Manes couple," she corrected.

"Yes."

"You want me to testify on behalf of your client."

"No."

"No?"

"No. And if you don't believe me, please phone Mr. Meyer yourself. He will corroborate my position. I don't think either of us should be obliged to testify in any way."

"So what are we doing here?"

"It is more serious than even you might realize. There's a possibility that Charles might be indicted and tried in Connecticut."

"So?"

"Connecticut has the death penalty."

Marion seemed unfazed by this news. However, she paused before saying: "What do you expect me to say?"

"I thought you might offer some suggestions. This predicament is new to me, though I'm sure an equal novelty for you."

I waited, hoping she might open up a bit.

"If there's anything you know that might shed some light on this situation, give me a clue as to what really might have happened—"

"You think he might have done it?" interrupted Marion.

"Yes," I nodded, "that is more than entirely possible." I sighed in an effort to organize my thoughts. "Given the particulars of their relationship, something I really only know from his point of view, I could see Charles being driven just beyond the point of good judgment. Driven to lash out at her and the frightful accusations she made."

"Such as?"

"Well, that he was impotent."

"He was. I'm certain of it."

I looked at Marion with an incredulity I usually save for the criminally insane, a category, as I have said before, I do not consider real. Their capacity to lie, however, is beyond any normal measure, so I prefer to call them "the criminally bizarre."

"Why do you think he married such an exhibitionist?"

At that precise moment, the waiter arrived with our steak and tuna salad sandwich. Marion remained unfazed and waited for my answer. After the waiter had departed, I quietly continued: "I certainly have my own estimate of their mismatch, but I'd be much more interested in yours."

"The man's a voyeur, J.C. You know that, don't you?"

This revelation could be embarrassing—that was my first thought. My second thought was how I might keep the depth of my ignorance a secret.

"A victim, yes. Perhaps a masochist even. But a voyeur?"

"Do you know how they met?"

"At a party. It was at Charlotte's and he had been invited."

"Yes, invited by a teammate who promised him plenty to look at."

"I beg your pardon."

"This was in the seventies, J.C. Swinging was not an uncommon phenomenon. Charlotte told me she had had a crush on Charles from watching him on television. A teammate whose name should not be recalled—"

"It may have to be."

"Be that as it may, he told Charlotte that Charles would agree to attend one of these parties if he could just watch."

Marion looked at me to see how things were registering thus far. I was far from inscrutable and in Marion's eyes an open book of titillated shame.

"She said fine if he came nude."

She left off and dug quite heartily into her still bloody steak.

"And that makes him a voyeur," I said rhetorically without the slightest hint of a question in it.

"No," she said between mouthfuls, "what he revealed then and in the years to come identified him as a voyeur."

I waited, knowing full well that she might leave me twisting slowly over my tuna salad sandwich for the entire time it took her to polish off a New York strip sirloin. I didn't mind. By now I had surrendered any moral high ground in this investigation. Marion was so much more interesting than any of the people we were talking about and my desire for her increased in direct proportion to the clarity she exhibited in this discussion.

"J.C.?"

She said this with the fulsome radiance of someone about to instruct another in the ABC's.

"Yes, Marion?"

"I am grateful for the speed with which you recommended Mrs. Manes to me. She had been in dire need of a woman therapist for years. Unfortunately, by the time she arrived at my doorstep there was little hope."

"You're sure of that."

"Yes. Her competitiveness was so thick that after seven months her resistance was barely breaking down. I can't say she clearly agreed to a contract from the start, but it was evident she had accepted my ground rules. But none of that seemed to help. She'd find new ways around the truth."

"And the truth was?"

"Her father had molested her. Severely. Took her on

long vacation trips to theme parks. There would be weeks at a time, in the same hotel room with him, back and forth to the beach and the restaurant, the clothing stores, the amusement parks, and all the while the culmination of each day was a session with Daddy."

Marion looked at me to see if I had registered how serious this was.

"It certainly didn't help that her mother was an abusive, fall-down drunk, and her father the typical mate for that, a wealthy pincushion that just waited for his time, postponed his pleasures until he could get Charlotte off somewhere."

"What do you mean by 'severely'?" I asked.

"She became addicted to it. Even after her father wanted to stop she realized that she had the power to bring him back to her. There'd be months where, after her parents divorced, he refused to see her. He would call her on the phone every few days or so. She would keep at him, using all kinds of sign language and code, sexual code. They had indulged in so many bizarre sessions together that almost anything was sexualized between them."

"How old was she?"

"When it started? Nine."

I found it very hard to remain seated. There we were in the Palm Court of the Plaza, a place where Charlotte's father might have taken her after a trip to F.A.O. Schwartz. They would enter, just the two of them, with their shopping bags dangling, and little Charlotte, very much the big little girl, very much Daddy's favorite, and very much looking forward to proving how happy she could make her father.

"'We don't need Mother,' is what Charlotte would say. 'All we need is each other.' Charlotte was very aware in our sessions of how culpable she was. Nine years old gave her no excuse. I tried to get her to talk about those feelings, the sense that she had seduced her father and wasn't entirely the victim, and she'd say, 'Of course, Miss Brockman'—that's how she referred to me, 'Miss Brockman,' never 'Doctor Brockman'—'I loved what I did to him. Drove him crazy. His guilt was a joy to me. He'd stand naked in front of me crying in shame and I would prove that part of him had no shame at all. I would make him as hard as your tabletop.'"

Marion's eyes were a bit too clear and glistening to put me at ease, but putting people at ease was never her strong suit.

"'Then I'd leave him on the bed after he made us both promise never to do it again.'"

I wasn't quite sure who was talking now—Marion or Charlotte.

"I would like dessert. How about you?"

XI

AFTER HEARING THAT I HAD indeed met with Marion, Mother leapt to the grand idea of a visit and announced she would arrive the following weekend.

"I'll see you on Friday," she said quietly. "The afternoon plane."

The weekend sprang all too abruptly upon me. Before I was prepared, there she was.

The taxi ride in from La Guardia was, as is common anywhere in the five boroughs of my city, a ghastly affair. The driver, a Middle Eastern terrorist no doubt, had chosen to bring his lunch with him in the car. The meal's aroma was more punitive than culinary.

"Shall we change cabs?" I suggested.

"No, J.C.," said Mother firmly, "I'm so rarely nauseated these days that I find this all a bit nostalgic. Carrying you made me almost as sick."

"How kind of you to tell me, Mother."

"How is Marion?"

"Fine," I said simply, feeling no compulsion to elaborate.

THE VOYEUR

The cab bounced along in its dreadful way for another two exit signs.

"That's all?" she added. "That's all I'm to hear?"

After a pause, I said: "Yes, Mother."

"Driver," she called to the front, "take me back to the airport."

"Now, Mother, hold on. Driver, continue into the city. I will tell you all about it, Mother, when we get home. All right?"

Mother chewed an invisible Southern cud for the next three exits.

"I'm too old, J.C., to be waiting about for the Truth. I don't care what the driver might overhear. He's probably daydreaming of the Twin Towers anyway."

"The meeting with Marion went as professionally as I could possibly expect, Mother!"

"How disappointing," she muttered. "Will you be seeing her again?"

"I'll be speaking to her on the phone, but aside from that, I have no idea what's in store."

Mother gazed into my eyes with infuriating compassion and then said: "Perhaps *I* should call her."

"No, Mother, God no," I implored. "Please don't do that."

She then looked at me for a long moment, as though trying to recognize me. "Are you sure?" she said quietly.

"Am I sure that I don't want my mother runnin' my affairs? Sexual or otherwise? Am I sure of that?! I am positive of that!"

Mother was smiling now. She had at last succeeded in getting me thoroughly vexed and upset.

Gripping my hand with both of hers, she whispered: "I'm so proud of you , son."

XII

Dooby, CHARLES MANES' BODYGUARD, WAS, much to my surprise, a mere six feet two inches tall. *My* height actually. The rest of his measurements, however, were not quite as convivial. I would venture to say he weighed in at roughly 240 pounds, not one ounce of which appeared to be mere flesh. His body had the density of lead, and if it weren't for his disarming and very childlike demeanor I would have ended the conversation as quickly as I had begun it. I had asked Charles' permission to question Dooby for my own edification, and Charles had most graciously consented. The meeting took place at a little coffee shop named PAX, on the corner of Fifty-seventh Street and Seventh Avenue.

"Oh, workin' for the Wizard's a cinch, piece o' cake, no hassle!"

Dooby said this while heaping into his generous mouth an impressive helping of fruit salad and yogurt sprinkled with wheat germ.

"He's workin' it all out," he continued. "I've got him on a better diet, too."

"Oh?" I offered.

"Yeah, very high protein, and a small workout with the

71

light weights. You don' wanna muscle-bound basketball player. Long, lean, 'n never mean's the ticket. Like Magic!"

"Mr. Johnson," I added.

"Yeah, he *is* the ticket!"

"You don't prefer Michael Jordan?"

"As a genius, sure, but as a basketball player? No, you need a friend, a playmaker, and a saint, a minor saint, nothin' *too* pure but just enough to keep the team on its toes. Someone to look up to."

"Well, Wizard is in almost as threatening a situation as Magic has found himself in."

"Oh, you mean the murder!"

"Yes," I said.

"Oh, he'll beat that."

He said this as if he'd been discussing a traffic ticket.

"Mr.—uh, I never did get your last name. . . ."

"Don't have one. Just Dooby."

"Well, Dooby, your certainty is refreshing. *I'm* not as confident. In fact, I quite fear for Mr. Manes' life. You *do* know the jurisdiction could be Connecticut."

"Yeah, the death penalty, I know, but he didn't do it."

"What makes you so positive about that?"

"I *know* the Wizard. He couldn't murder the *other* wizards."

"I beg your pardon?"

"In a battle with a herd of Ku Kluxers, he'd be the first to wanna sit down 'n talk."

"Oh, well," I murmured while collecting my rebuttal, "*I* know him in a way you may not."

"Oh, no, Dr. Kaminer, I've seen the Wiz under every pressure imaginable. Forgive me, but your little office doesn't *have* a hot seat like the NBA playoffs or a mobster's invitation to negotiate. In all that time, he never got angry. He was in pain but every time the Pistons gave him a cheap shot in the box or Charlie C. started with the offers—"

"Charlie C.?"

"Wiz tol' me you knew about the point-shaving offer 'n everything—"

"Yes."

"Well, Charlie C. arranged the whole thing. He's pretty big. Not too far from Gotti's neighborhood, if you catch my drift."

I nodded my increasingly alarmed comprehension. By now we were standing on the street just outside of PAX.

"Is there," I asked, "any possibility of further trouble with this Mr. C.?"

"*I* don't think so," said Dooby with a shrug, "but Wiz wants to keep me around, says I'm good luck. I tell him *you* are, Doctor. You *know* his game point average just shot up when he tied up with you."

"I know all too well," I added eagerly. "It is my fondest dream to see him nudge Mr. Air Jordan right out of his complacent little Nikes."

Dooby laughed a great laugh, then offered his hand for a high five which I responded to as gracefully as my Southern reserve would allow.

"Michael's leavin'!"

"What?" I asked.

"Michael Jordan's gonna quit."

He paused to see the effect of his pronouncement.

"That's the rumor," he continued. "S'posed to have a press conference 'bout it tomorrow. If he goes, the field'll be wide open!"

I pondered the sad irony of a wide open field and Charles Manes trapped in jail.

"Do you have any idea who *might* have killed Charlotte Manes, or even who would have wanted to?"

Dooby grew pensive for the first time in our conversation. "The list is so long, Doctor, I don't know if we have the time," he said after a pause.

I took a moment to absorb the certainty of this indictment. "Did she have any *friends*, Dooby?"

Dooby thought a moment. "Her mother."

"Her mother?"

He nodded and then, with a very raised eyebrow: "And that's it!"

"What about her father?" I asked, not without a certain twinge of embarrassment.

"Her father?!"

Dooby practically spat the words, then looked at me as if I had just expressed undying admiration for Jefferson Davis.

"Yes," I said, "what about him?"

Dooby's look dropped away and for the first time he seemed uncomfortable. "I've just heard bad things about him."

"Yes?" I encouraged.

"Yeah, like he mistreated her and stuff."

"Oh," I responded, "really."

"Yeah, they didn't see each other much."

"Have you ever met him?" I asked.

"No, I don't think even the Wiz has."

"And her mother?"

"Oh, we've all met her," he said with an actorly gesture and expression more befitting news of Mr. Hyde than a determinedly loving mother.

"What do you think of her?"

"She's the boss. No doubt about that."

I waited a moment hoping he might elaborate, but he didn't. "Do you think her father might have killed her?" I prodded.

"Oh, I don't know, that goes a long way back."

"You mean the abuse."

"Yeah."

"How'd you hear about the abuse?"

Dooby suddenly seemed evasive. "I don't know, rumors maybe."

"Ahhh," I offered, "so you've heard it from several different sources."

He nodded quite indecisively.

"Did you like Charlotte Manes?"

He looked at me strangely and then shook his head. "No, I didn't like the way she treated the Wizard."

"I am doing my best, Dooby, to exonerate your boss, to keep him, if not out of jail, at least out of the electric chair.

75

If you think of anything that might help me, I would appreciate your contacting me as quickly as possible."

"Sure, Doc, you got it."

Upon that strangely simplified response we high-fived again and parted.

XIII

MOTHER WAS IN THE KITCHEN when I returned from the meeting with Dooby.

"What're you doin'?" I asked.

"Cookin'," she replied coyly.

"Mother, I told you I'd made dinner reservations at Le Chantilly."

"Cancel them," she said firmly but sweetly. "I don't get the urge to cook often and we'd all better take advantage of it."

I sniffed the air. "Chicken?" I asked.

"Pollo contadino," she sang in her Southern Italian voice. Her "Delta Dago," as she calls it.

"All right," I sighed as I turned toward the living room and the phone.

After canceling our reservations and taking off my jacket and tie, I returned to the living room to find Mother standing there with a glass of Lillet in her hand. She held it out to me.

"There you are, son!"

"Thank you, Mother," I said suspiciously.

"The comforts of home, son. You should get more accustomed to the comforts of a *real* environment."

She sat on the chair nearest the front window. It looked out on the vast stretches of Central Park.

"I haven't questioned the *reality* of my existence, Mother. Aside from an infuriating few hours in the philosophy classes of Dartmouth, I don't ever recall thinking of my life as a dream."

"Perhaps you should try it," she murmured dreamily as she stared out at Manhattan.

"Can I get *you* a drink, Mother?"

"No, I'm cookin'. Cookin' and drinkin' is a little like drivin' and drinkin'. It could prove disastrous for the other fellow."

I sat and sipped at my Lillet for a few blissful minutes. Such moments of familial calm were rare between us. Mother actually looked happy.

"Well," I questioned, "what canaries have you been into today?"

She turned coyly in my direction with a kind of mischief only Southern inbreeding could have spawned and announced: "I called Marion."

I rose instantly. "You didn't!" I cried.

"I did," she sighed.

"You witch!"

She laughed.

I strode about the room looking for some suitable corner to throw my drink into.

"It was very brief, J.C.," she said. "The whole matter was over in minutes."

78

"The whole matter?!" I cried. "And what whole matter are we talkin' about?!"

After turning her head in that slightly ruffled admission of guilt, she said: "I invited her to lunch."

My head began to twist in silent noes.

"I'm seein' her tomorrow."

I began to moan. Words seemed utterly inadequate.

"And it won't be at the Palm Court."

XIV

SUNDAYS ARE A STRANGELY LABORIOUS day of rest, as if the week's efforts were a careless duty compared to the call of the Sabbath. Herds of people bustle toward their churches to kneel before a statue, open their mouths like fuzzy little hatchlings, eat what they believe to be the body of a god, sip a wine they prefer not to think of as blood though their god told them it is, and then return to their pews in some abject surrender to either their good intentions or the hideous thoughts they've been carrying with them all week.

I watch them carefully from *outside* their cathedrals. I am utterly convinced their Lord either fell one step short of the truth or His disciples refused to emphasize a discovery only the Book of John reveals:

> *In the beginning*
> *was The Word*
> *and*
> *The Word*
> *was God.*

That is *my* church.

My temple.

The Word.

Has been for quite a few years.

And not just one word but all words.

I'm literally carried by them through my day.

When asked my religion, I reply: "Word Bearer. It is my one and only obligation under God or Godlessness."

Think of all the words you might use to describe God. Any god. Any divinity. They all apply equally to words. Words are invisible. They are ubiquitous. They are, in their entirety, omniscient. They are eternal. When formed in our hearts they are as mysterious and indomitable as any Greek or Roman deity. And when picked up in the battle of truth, a mere selection of five may lead 620,000 men to their deaths.

"All men are created equal" proved to be not only the fiercest tool in Abraham Lincoln's arsenal, but that phrase's continuing mystery and power have raised its author, Thomas Jefferson, in my eyes, to biblical proportions. In the same way the Golden Rule and the Sermon on the Mount shrank the message of the Old Testament into Christ's own unified field theory, eight syllables have condensed Jesus' discovery, have simplified the entire New Testament into five words.

If I have any doubts? Confront any moral dilemmas?

Five words, eight syllables, spring to my assistance:

All men
are

created
equal.

Suddenly action, both fierce and friendly, invades me with calm and utter certainty. Enemies and battle companions alike are swiftly identified and the clarion call of war sounds.

Are they the words of God?

Nope.

The words themselves are my God.

And like a stone in David's sling, I hurl that phrase and its offspring, my verbal variations on that theme, fire them at my enemies.

"Words. Words, words, words."

It was Hamlet's tragedy to have uttered that phrase in despair.

All words for me are not only a joyful noise unto the Lord itself. They are my Lord. My God. My Destiny.

Why they should carry me *that* day, that Sunday afternoon, by St. Patrick's Cathedral is still unclear. Mother had chosen to lunch with Marion at Rumpelmayer's. It was a suitable compromise between two sensibilities utterly divided by that great cultural canyon known as Fifth Avenue.

The East Side of Manhattan and the West Side of Manhattan both spawn creatures intelligent but completely at war with each other over what is required to live a meaningful life.

The East Side of Manhattan is silk.

The West is tweed and denim.

Fifth Avenue apartment buildings have foyers the size of hotel lobbies.

West of Central Park the doormen simply point, and do so on a first-name basis.

An East Sider's aesthetic is French.

The West Sider's philosophy? Italian.

Scurrying between these polar appetites race the lust for adventure, the tenacities of hope, and New York City's increasing thirst for wine. Recent pronouncements on the holistic properties of the fermented grape have not only made sommeliers busier but both sides of Fifth Avenue smugly ecstatic over the heart-strengthening properties of a wine-inspired high.

A votre santé is not only pronounced more accurately these days but uttered with complete and absolute medicinal conviction.

Mother and Marion could very well have been exerting themselves in Dionysian aerobics at that very moment. And doing it in perfect East Side–West Side summitry.

The traditional café of the St. Moritz Hotel offers an East Side ambiance with a West Sider's sense of practicality and the questionable victory of being located just one block west of Fifth Avenue.

I had no idea, as I strolled by Rockefeller Plaza, what the two of them had envisioned for their meeting, either separately or together.

Mother
is a matchmaker

> *and knows*
> *for certain*
> *that I'm running*
> *out of time.*

The phrase almost seemed a suitable lyric for some Broadway musical or other, and so its singsong rhythms repeated their beat incessantly as I watched the married couples exit St. Patrick's Cathedral.

Their children were grasped firmly by the hand and benignly dragged to some destination or other. The eyes of their parents carried neither joy nor despair. Most seemed filled with the obligations of their next appointment, be it a Sunday feast or only a dull trip home to their television sets.

Could I ever be one of them?

Could the timeworn rituals of family life, even in the 1990s, offer some novelty to one so bereft of a family?

To put it plainly, I had been born a bastard. There is no other word for it really. The harshness of its ring completes the nature of its creation. Lust, pure and simple, had led to my conception. I was stung to life by sin and sinful I would remain till some Christian thought it fit to give me a name other than my mother's. And whether he did it out of lust or loving good intentions wouldn't matter one iota. The arc of his sexual organ wouldn't effect my future so long as the bent of his pen was to sign me into dignity, to endorse some contract or other between himself and my mother.

Nothing of the sort had ever ensued and I had lived in

shameless shamefulness, a kind of haughty self-defense, for most of my existence. Whatever pain accompanies this upbringing has its salutary side. The ache and long- ing of aloneness provokes a much deeper faith in life than the easy and glibly exchanged assurances of law and social convention. Bastardy had become my own no- ble and emboldening scarlet letter.

Mother had made no efforts to conceal the matter from me. From my earliest days, I remember her saying: "Child of love, J.C., you are the brazen child of my heart and soul and body and don't you forget that!"

When I asked what had happened to my father, she simply said: "Not the marrying sort, J.C. He was just not the marrying sort."

Apparently I had been conceived in New York, of all places. In Manhattan, during my mother's efforts to live here as an artist, a portrait painter. Of course Grampa Kaminer saw to it she never went without, but when he heard of her pregnancy he rushed her home immediately and set her up in the back room of the Kaminer home- stead.

"When I began to show," said Mother, "when your re- ality began to enforce itself on Papa's eyes, he sent me with Mother to Florida. You were born in April, so it seemed to one and all in Bremington that I'd simply been vacationing."

She paused here. It was the classic Kaminer pause.

"Until, of course, it became apparent that I was not go- ing to give you up."

At this point she smiled. "Your screams from my bedroom used to alarm my bridge partners. 'What the devil is that?' they'd ask, all prim and proper in their lies. And Persephone would go running by us to the stairs. 'That's my child,' I'd say simply and they'd laugh."

"Soon there was no more laughter and eventually no more bridge partners except for Emily Louise Davis, who was just too stupid to comprehend anything. I used to call her Rover, she was so loyal and unquestioning."

As the memory of Mother's revelations arose in me, I wondered whether she was also telling the same tale to Marion over a nice bottle of Meursault.

I didn't think it would matter much to Marion whether I was legitimate or not. Little did I know that Mother had other news for Marion this day—information that belonged to no one but herself and me. That she had neglected to tell her own son and chose to confess the facts to Marion first was something I would not become aware of until the very last days of this story. There's a fairly obvious explanation for my mother's oversight. My knowledge of these secrets might inevitably seal a vow of mine to never marry.

XV

Even when we were at the airport and waiting for the four o'clock plane, Mother refused to divulge her conversation with Marion.

"We ladies have our own vows of confidentiality," she said as she kissed me on the cheek, and then turned toward the gate, entering its chute swiftly and without looking back.

That evening I had a single ticket to one of my favorite entertainments: Carnegie Hall. The New York Philharmonic under the baton of Kurt Masur. This symphony's previous conductor, despite my rabid devotion to New York City, had left me so dissatisfied that I had canceled my subscription. It left me comfortably busy with my regular seats to Carnegie Hall—the Great Orchestra Series. Fortunately, the series afforded me a glimpse of Maestro Masur. Before I regale you with the inspired meditations I experienced under the spell of his not entirely unblack magic, I must reveal the auspicious encounter I faced while dining alone—which is my usual wont—at a favorite watering hole of mine, Gallagher's Steakhouse on Fifty-second Street.

I entered with typically warm anticipations. I know most of the headwaiters and all of the bartenders with whom I carry on a precarious deliberation over the devil drink. It is there I have both triumphed and failed in my not-so-midlife path toward abstinence. No, I have not succeeded. My hope is that, as it did my uncle Henry, old age will slow me down in such a way as to lessen my intake accordingly, though I have no intention of carrying this vow, as he did, to the confessional halls of Alcoholics Anonymous.

At any rate, this particular evening I measured my drink impeccably. Beginning with a Campari and soda, a libation so harmless as to almost not be included in my inventory of intoxicants, I commenced toward a very nice *half*-bottle of Château Simard's Saint Emilion. With the very healthy ballast of Gallagher's breadsticks and salt rolls, a nicely chopped salad of onions and perfect New Jersey tomatoes, a deliciously medium-rare chopped steak with the restaurant's famous sauce—the whole evening almost a mere excuse to drink the stuff straight out of the bowl—and a large bottle of Evian water to dilute not only the alcohol but the tons of death-dealing salt contained in every morsel of this monstrous diversion all simultaneously assaulting my taste buds and metabolism, I seemed to keep the side effects to a minimum. I also did *not* wish to absorb the efforts of a master conductor on the darker side of inebriation. Maestro Masur would be assured of my complete and most willing attentions.

As I was conducting a debate with my waiter, a very

portly fellow named Robust, on the relative merits of the female versus the male lobster—he preferred the male, huge and impressively meaty, while I savor the tender offerings of the deceptively more fragile side of the partnership—we were most rudely interrupted by a Lieutenant William Bridey of the N.Y.P.D., a regular of this establishment and, I'm sorry to say, one of the more doubtfully fine among New York's Finest.

"Hello, Kaminer," he slurred. "*Doctor* Kaminer. I'm sorry."

"That's quite all right, Lieutenant, I'm often confused about such titles myself."

"No yer not. Yer jus' fulla shit." He smiled. "*Smooth* shit. You got the smoothest shit 'n the city."

"I'm flattered to hear you say that."

"Can I sit down?"

"Well, I'm off to Carnegie Hall in about five minutes—"

"Tha's all it'll take."

I nodded. He sat.

"I shouldn't be telling you this, but the Wizard's gettin' a raw deal so I thought it might help ya to know there's another suspect."

One of the more fortunate and *un*fortunate eventualities of a convivial drinking establishment is that any prolonged patronage will quickly reveal your most highly profiled achievements and disasters. My success with the Wizard, so graciously shared with the world by Mr. Manes himself, left me a minor celebrity in a ten-block piece of Manhattan real estate more filled with celebrity than any similarly sized patch of extravagance in Hollywood. This explains why Lieutenant Bridey knew of my profession and, at least in this case, one of my clients.

I had hoped Lieutenant Bridey would just continue, would simply give me the name of this suspect and leave. But no, he preferred to play hide-and-seek.

"May I ask, Lieutenant, to whom you might be referring?"

"Yer not gonna believe this."

"I fear I may *have* to."

"Charlotte Manes' father, George Benedict."

I stared at him for a bit and then the inevitable "Hmmm" arose from my lips.

"Hmmmm is right, Doc!"

"Is there a motive?"

"She was tellin' everyone he fucked her."

This was delivered in a very broad whisper.

Though surprised, it didn't take me long to realize any delay in my reply might give this caveman the victory he had come for, the prize of having shocked a psychiatrist with the *real* facts of life, those items only experienced and understood by officers of the law.

"And who, may I ask, is everyone?" I asked with a slight smile.

"The head of surgery at Zion Hospital."

I couldn't think of an institution further from the world of Charlotte Manes than a Jewish hospital for geriatrics.

"Actually, he heard it from the nurses."

"*All* of them?"

Bridey smiled. "No, Doc. But enough of 'em."

"How did all of this get to the police?'

"Goldman, the surgeon at Zion, dropped the information on the commissioner at a special mayor's meeting about 'racial tensions.'"

Bridey put quotes around "racial tensions" with his eyebrows.

"Have you arrested Charlotte's father?"

"No, but he was questioned and he sounds real vague on his whereabouts that day."

"What do I owe you for this rather depressing information?"

"Depressing?! It might get the Wizard off."

"It might. But my instincts tell me Charlotte's father is no more guilty than Charles Manes, and these recent revelations, which are bound to get to the press, will destroy the man."

Bridey gave me a particularly disturbing smile. "Oh? You feelin' sorry for pederasts?"

"I feel sorry for us all, Mr. Bridey, present company particularly, and, if you'll excuse me, I must leave for my concert. They lock the doors throughout the first movement and I wouldn't like to miss it."

As I left the table I could hear him muttering, "Pompous shithead."

XVI

TCHAIKOVSKY IS NOT A COMPOSER I particularly care for. The depth of self-pity in some of his melodies can be infuriating. His own estimate of his Fifth Symphony as "fabricated" and "insincere" is, I think, not without merit. However, in the hands of Maestro Kurt Masur these little pathodies become the frantically exciting outbursts of a very gifted delirium. Mr. Masur's facial eruptions and the cuneiform ballets his hands construct on the podium project a most endearing madness. Of course, from the audience you can't share in the mischief of his eyes or the depth of his self-containment when the profounder portions of a composition are reached. When that occurs, the prayer begins and unless you are utterly without any redeeming social value, you can't help but fall to your own spiritual intimacies.

This detailed information about his face I gleaned while watching the maestro on TV. Clearly a man quite comfortable with the tyranny of his demons. Those which the music unleashes will train their energies on the roughly one hundred gifted grazers that feed so safely beneath his baton. The invisible furies seem to leap from his eyes and quivering hands and go racing into the articulators of what is, of course, the greatest instrument the world has ever known, the symphony orchestra. I have learned, however, that without the distinct and tyrannous particulars of a single individual of genius, mind you, in short, a Kurt Masur, to lead this miracle through the steps of a masterpiece, you really have nothing to leave home for.

With all of this in mind, I entered Carnegie Hall anticipating a challenge. Would the image of Kurt Masur's face be satisfactorily balanced by the energies of his orchestra? Much to my surprise, all of these anticipations led me to a prolonged meditation on the particulars of the Charlotte Manes murder, the mystery of the death of P. I. Tchaikovsky, and most of all, the unspeakable horror now confronting Charlotte Manes' father. All of these themes whirling about amid the vast canvas of the Tchaikovsky Fourth Symphony.

Can our sins be gracefully borne if their origins make it impossible to trust yourself with even your smallest breath? It is the voyeur's privilege to unlock not only the lust within each expression but the agony as well. During the progress of Tchaikovsky's musical secret-telling, the following question arose within me, the most committed of voyeurs: How can a Czarist Russian homosexual feel any more accepted in his world than an exposed incestuite?

And down there on the stage was that madman, Maestro Masur. His twitching left hand and the delicate frenzies of his right moving quite gracefully within that glorious confessional, guiding its disclosures like a tightly contained dervish, his eyes all widened by the energies and his face shaking in the frenzy of the composer's confession of so many notes, so many hungers, so many hurts, so many lusts, so many demands, so many terrors, so many insults, so many embarrassing nights, so many guarded obscenities, and shame, shame, shame all the while creeping throughout the exultation, thrusting its lurid little hands into the few hidden corners left, Tchaikovsky unburdened of any obligation to feel sorry for himself. Just all of the tingling perils and protestations of the pot which would demand of the Potter,

Why
have you made me
this way?!

And coming up with the answer, if ever so briefly, that he is what he is, and that, hopefully, someday in the perhaps distant future, all of those unique absurdities contained in his truth will be entrusted to the hands of an unapologetic maestro. Someone who will celebrate the pains that could very well have driven the poet to suicide.

As for the alleged pedophile, Mr. George Benedict, what solace could there even be in sleep, if waking could only mean a deeper terror of an even more detailed exposure?

At the intermission, I entered the hall's own café and browsed through the program while sipping my second Campari and soda of the evening. As I was adjusting my high like the volume on a very sensitive tape deck, who should cross the nicely renovated room but my very own Dr. Marion Brockman.

"J.C."

"Marion!" I exclaimed as I pondered how complete Mother's report on my Sunday whereabouts might have been. Could Ms. Brockman have sought me out this evening?

"I can't think of a lovelier coincidence," I cooed, "than you entering the present circle of my thoughts and in such a perfectly shaded evocation of summer blue skies."

She indeed was conservatively provocative in her summer blue suit with the slightly peek-a-boo paisley blouse that crept out from under the almost severe cut of her jacket.

Why not brave the stormy sea, I thought to myself. "How was your meeting with my mother?" I asked, diving in.

Marion paused to stare directly into my eyes.

"Confidential, J.C. Entirely confidential."

I gazed rather shamelessly at the front of her suit and then down at her exquisitely turned ankles. She had, perhaps, the best pair of legs in all of Manhattan.

"J.C., you're high," she said with a smile.

Only she would have recognized the fine differences I had constructed in my evening's modified abandon.

"How comforting to know," I said, "that there's little I can hide from you. Or care to."

"If I weren't escorted this evening," she continued with the same smile, "I might enjoy the challenge of sobering you up."

After recovering from the excitement of that possibility, I looked around to determine who her escort might be.

"He's over there, J.C."

She pointed in the direction of the coffee counter. There, looking directly at us, was a disturbingly handsome young man at least seven to ten years Marion's junior. Before I could say a word, Marion said happily: "One of my students." Marion conducts a postgraduate course in diagnosis at NYU, part of the doctoral program.

"Is that allowed?" I asked.

"It's not very professional, J.C., but it has been known to happen."

"It's terrible what old age'll do to us, Marion."

"I beg your pardon," she offered quietly, as the young annoyance approached with two cups of coffee. Young, in this instance, meant roughly late twenties/early thirties.

"J.C., this is Arnold Betleiter. Arnold, J. C. Kaminer."

After giving Marion her coffee, he offered his free hand to me.

"Pleasure to meet you, Doctor. I recognized you earlier. Actually, I pointed you out to Marion. It's a privilege to meet you. I'm an admirer of your essays particularly."

"Then you are older than you appear, young man," I said. "I haven't published one in years."

"That's what's fun about you, Doctor. Hunting the stacks for all of your old opinions."

I looked at Marion who shrugged blithely with lidded eyes.

"You realize that you are escorting one of the brightest therapeutic lights west of Central Park!" I declared.

"And east of the Hudson!"

There had been a longtime feud between us over the relative integrity of living west or east of Fifth Avenue. Her early pro bono days had convinced her that any physician with Park or Fifth Avenue connections was suspect. I, of course, immediately upon arriving in Manhattan had chosen the most affordably expensive address I could find. It still bewilders her that I remain as attractive to her as I do. Our one passionate weekend together was spent watching her eyes widen in disbelief at the weakness of her own scruples. I would have given anything this evening to immediately pick up where we had left off. Mother would have been proud.

After listening to the young man ingratiate himself to both of us in a mildly disgusting way, I thought I would throw down a slightly velvet gauntlet.

"Young man," I ventured, "following this concert it would be the greatest honor if you would allow *me* to escort Dr. Brockman home—"

Marion's head actually jerked in amazement at my gall. "J.C., you're preposterous and growing more foolish each day. Arnold, let's leave J.C. to his drink and return to our seats."

With mild but obvious discomfort, Arnold, after excusing himself, did as he was told. The two departed into the concert hall leaving me to savor the abrupt end of my fantasies.

I have grown old, I thought. Very unpersuasive. Downright awkward I was. With that I left Carnegie Hall entirely and ventured home in a cab.

There awaiting me was the voice of Marion Brockman on my phone recorder: "J.C., I'm worried about you. Aren't there better ways to pass your time than making such a fool of yourself? Call me tomorrow. Perhaps we can meet at my office."

How splendid, I thought. She made that phone call immediately after leaving me. She went off to a pay phone before the second half began and left that wonderfully concerned insult on my tape.

After a small glass of beer—I keep the six-ounce bottles freezing cold for just such occasions—I retired to bed with a very excited smile on my face.

XVII

"Hello."

"Marion?"

At the sound of my voice, her warm, cordial tone turned glacial, the kind of icy horizon you'd wish only on polar bears and Joseph Stalin.

"Dr. Kaminer."

"You can call me 'Mister' if you'd like."

There followed a slight pause during which the north winds seemed to blow miraculously into one of my ears and out the other, having had no discernible effect upon my own desire to invade Marion Brockman like some warm, Caribbean breeze.

"Don't you think your flippancy has angered me enough?"

"It seems to be the only way I can get your attention."

"Is that what you want?"

"Yes. Hasn't that been obvious?"

"Then I will most gladly oblige. See me at my office this afternoon."

"I'm sorry, Marion, but I've appointments all day. Perhaps dinner."

"No, my office or nowhere."

"Then tomorrow."

"Fine."

"What time?"

"Five P.M. And don't be late."

"No, ma'am."

Click went the end of the line.

Hmmmmm, I mused. Five o'clock. End of the day. Her last appointment. Hmmmmmm.

XVIII

EARLY THE NEXT DAY THE phone range. It was Mother.

"J.C., I hope I woke you."

"Yes, you did, Mother."

"Was Marion at Carnegie Hall the other night?"

"Yes, Mother. Courtesy of your little information highway, I'm sure."

"No," corrected Mother quickly. "She had announced her plans for the evening before I even mentioned yours, and lo and behold, fate drew you both together."

"You expect me to believe that?"

"No," she said simply.

"Don't grow inscrutable on me now, Mother. Just what have you been up to?"

"Watering my Indian pipes," she said. "What did you think of her young boyfriend?"

"She told you about him?!"

"Of course she did. How else was she to make you jealous?"

"Oh," I answered. "You think she intended that for me?"

"I certainly do."

"Then why didn't you tell me at the airport?"

"You might have changed your plans, avoided her entirely, and I want you jealous, J.C.," she said. "I want you to consider seriously what you may have thrown away."

"Hmmmm," I sang into the phone.

"Hmmm indeed, J.C.," echoed Mother.

I looked at the clock. It was 7:00 A.M.

"Mother, do you realize what time it is here?"

"Same time it is here. I couldn't sleep and so it seemed only sensible to not let you sleep either. My hopes for you and Marion have quite discombobulated my schedule."

"Now, hold on, Mother. What hopes are you talking about?"

"Marriage."

She paused for my reaction.

I gave her none.

"Marriage and children." Again she paused. "I refuse to see the Kaminer name die with you."

"Mother, by the time a child of mine reached college, I'd be close to seventy."

"And I'd be ninety-five, J.C."

"They'd be feeding both of us through a tube, Mother."

"Not me, J.C. I plan on enjoying my grandchildren."

XIX

MY APPOINTMENTS WITH CHARLES MANES were, as always, scheduled bright and early. The time had been conceived as a way of assuring Charles a full day. He had, before encountering me, been prone to lie about in bed all day until practice—much to his late wife's dismay—or if it were the off-season, to just lie about for twenty-four hours. He had, aside from the distractions Charlotte would coax him to, no life outside of basketball. Since our first appointment, however, he had not only taken to rising earlier but had developed a number of other interests as well: cars (he had purchased a new Mercedes 500 SL) and children (he had become a regular instructor at the Harlem Boys Club). And writing. Taking a tip from his own instructor, Charles had taken to keeping a journal and even constructing a few poems now and then.

This morning, however, he was in an almost frightening condition. He obviously hadn't slept a wink and I sensed that perhaps he had been drinking. I was hardly one to lecture him on addiction or any other substantive abuse of himself, but this development was new and dis-

103

turbing. Charles' problems until this day had been purely psychic. His living habits, generally, appeared to be healthy.

"Charles?"

"Yes," he mumbled.

"You look terrible. What have you been doing?"

He seemed relieved that I had noticed and proceeded to lie down on the couch.

"I've been out drinking."

"Yes?" I encouraged.

"I don't use cocaine—thank God—and I've never really had a bad habit except, as you so frankly say, being a professional victim."

"I said you have 'behaved as one.' There's a difference."

He looked at me from his prone position and smiled. "Yeah, I know, instilling hope in me, right? Not letting me face facts? Pulling out the old power of positive thinking?"

"Don't take it personally. I not only do it with all of my patients, I do it with myself as well and if you believe in me at all it's probably because of that. I am certain, if you will forgive my presumption, that I project an affirmative attitude toward life. Is that true or not?"

He looked away for a bit and then conceded flatly: "Yeah, I guess so."

I waited. This was a child now. Before me on the couch lay a ten- or twelve-year-old giant, a boy utterly lost in the world of a new school. He had played with the wrong children, they had influenced him badly, he knew it and didn't know how to assure himself that it would never happen again.

"Doctor?"

"Yes."

"Have you ever thought of suicide?"

Hmmmmm, I thought, so it's arrived, the victim's ace in the hole.

There are, in every therapist's life, certain classic moments we all dread equally. The most vivid is the first time a client pulls out the word "suicide" or familiar euphemisms like "escape" or "rest," or the common phrases like "I'm tired of life, Doctor," or "It gets just too much to bear sometimes." The last one must be repeated numerous times before a physician's warning bell is obliged to go off. Charles Manes' bold entrance through the front door with the word itself was a little startling but not entirely unexpected. My response was practiced.

"Everyone does, Charles, but what are your *own* particular thoughts?"

"I don't think I could do it."

What a welcome relief it was to hear that. Clearly, the Wizard could never have been more pinned to the wall than at that moment, and if after perhaps an all-night drinking fest his resources helped him come up with such a simple acceptance of his will to live, I thought there might be a blessing in disguise in all this disaster.

"What makes you think that?" said I, trying to conceal my satisfaction.

"I tried."

He looked at me when he said it.

"And I failed."

I nodded to myself and then added: "Obviously."

"I turned the gas on in our apartment." He paused.

"There is no 'our apartment,' is there, Doctor?"

"No, Charles."

"Well, I turned it on and when I got a little sick to my stomach and headachey, I thought, this is what she wants. She'd be very happy if I were dead. And I didn't want to do that, you know, give her that satisfaction."

Charles lay there in silence contemplating the certainty of his statement. I, however, was bewildered.

"Charles, despite your wife's unfortunate behavior toward you, I never sensed that she hated you. I know that may sound strange, but those kinds of emotions are very clear and I really doubt whether she would have wanted you dead."

"Not Charlotte, Doctor. I'm not talking about her. It's her mother. Charlotte's mother wanted me dead the minute she laid eyes on me."

XX

THE BENEDICT FAMILY, CHARLOTTE'S FAMILY, were third-generation and mildly well-to-do Connecticut gentry. Charlotte's mother lived not far from the small town of Ridgefield on one of those modest estates that are not quite large but not exactly small. Certainly not ostentatious, since it was well hidden behind elms and oaks. There were none of those wall-sized shrubs about, the ones so common to the larger mansions in the Hamptons. No, one approached the house by a circular driveway which threaded past trees and an unselfconsciously yet well-tended front lawn. The day of my visit I sensed that a mowing was slightly overdue.

Mrs. Benedict herself opened the door.

"Dr. Kaminer?"

"Yes," I offered as I tried to hold my smile through the onslaught of her examination. The woman didn't so much look at you as interrogate you with her eyes. Sensing the mental acuity behind those eyes, it was hard to believe that she could be unaware of the relationship between her husband and Charlotte.

"Come in," she said abruptly. "This won't take long, will it?"

"No," I suggested vaguely, not wanting to pin down the time.

"I understand that you were responsible for Charlotte finding Dr. Brockman," she said.

"Partly, yes."

"Well, it is because of *that* I'm willing to see you. Your connection to Charles, of course, is certainly not in your favor."

"That's what I wanted to talk to you about."

By now we were in the living room.

"Please, be seated."

I sat on the couch while she sat in a straight-backed chair, quite obviously determined to brave this interview without comfort.

"There's nothing to talk about. He's a *Negro*," she said forcefully. "He married my daughter. I'm white and I'm prejudiced."

I sensed immediately how quickly Mrs. Benedict wanted to end this. "So there's nothing personal?"

"What do you mean?"

"Well, prejudice is a pretty general state of affairs. Do you mean there was nothing about Charles in particular that you hated?"

"He was a basketball player. Why would I *ever* want to get involved with a sport like that?"

"Like what, Mrs. Benedict?"

"Please, Doctor, don't stoke my fires here. I'm angry. Angry about a lot of things. Charlotte's death is a major source of my anger, but it doesn't stop there. It takes very little to set me off these days and I certainly don't want to go off on a harangue about the disgusting world of Negroes and basketball."

She looked about herself in great impatience. Her hands clasped nervously in front of her.

"I understand," I said, rising from the couch. "You are obviously in a great deal of pain and I am not about to put you through any more at this time."

She seemed surprised at the abrupt end to my questions.

"If you will excuse me," I continued, "I will call at a later date. Perhaps we can—"

"Well, you needn't leave *this* quickly."

"I am trying to find out who killed your daughter, Mrs. Benedict, and—"

"Charles did!"

"I'm not so sure."

"It's obvious," she went on a little helplessly.

"No, Mrs. Benedict, I don't think so. Your daughter had many enemies, so many that it can never be quite that simple."

"Well, George certainly wasn't one of them."

"Your husband?"

"My *ex*-husband."

"You know he's a suspect?"

"Yes, the police called yesterday to ask about him. It's preposterous. I mean, what possible reason could he have?"

Mrs. Benedict spoke these words with such innocence

that it took my breath away. What an awful revelation it'll be, I thought, if she's truly as unaware as she appears of the history between her husband and her daughter.

"The police mentioned no motive?" I asked.

"No, they said they'd need to talk to me privately, so they're coming here."

"Today?"

"Yes, this afternoon. I insisted it be in the afternoon so I could recover from whatever questions *you* might have asked me."

She again began taking her nervous little looks about the room.

I wasn't sure what to do. Certainly the police were going to inform her of her husband's incest with Charlotte. I debated whether to just leave and let the harsher forces invade her little world or to broach the subject myself. Then it occurred to me that Mrs. Benedict must have some respectful feelings toward Marion Brockman.

"Mrs. Benedict? You mentioned Dr. Brockman."

"Yes."

"Did Charlotte speak to you about her?"

"Mentioned her once, said she was seeing her. Since that time Charlotte seemed to gain some sense. At least she didn't look as crazy. I assumed it was Dr. Brockman's influence."

"Quite possibly it was, Mrs. Benedict."

I turned toward the door, still unsure of what to do.

"You may call me Polly," she said tensely.

I turned back. She smiled so shyly and the little girl within her was so painfully apparent, I felt like a father

110

about to tell his daughter that there was not only no Santa Claus but that St. Nick could possibly be up on charges of molesting the children in his lap.

"Mrs. Benedict—Polly—I'm fairly certain about what the police are going to tell you and it's not pleasant. It's quite disturbing, in fact. I really don't know what to do since I'm privy to information about your family in some very indirect ways. You may very well be aware of this, I don't know."

"Aware of what?"

"I am in a very awkward position. Professionally it is a little compromising. I have taken to a bit of sleuthing to try and help my client, but I see how complicated it gets. Would you do this for me? Would you call Dr. Brockman yourself? I will have spoken to her and I think she would prove immensely helpful in this situation. You really should talk to her first."

"Doctor, you're scaring me." She said this quite clearly and simply. "I am not going to go through some wait-and-see game with two strangers such as you and Dr. Brockman in order to somehow protect myself from a pack of even greater strangers. Out with it, Doctor."

After a badly disguised sigh, I began. "Did Charlotte ever speak to you about her relationship with her father?"

"They didn't get along."

She said this so quickly and with such certainty that I knew the news I had for her would be shocking.

"As far as I know they hadn't seen each other for years," she added.

111

"Apparently that is not the case," I began slowly. "And this is something she certainly disclosed to her therapist, Dr. Brockman, because I heard about it from her. Your daughter also seems to have disclosed it to other people as well."

"What are you talking about?"

"They had an affair."

It came out of me simply and almost boldly. I too had grown sick of my evasions and the phrase just blurted out.

It seemed to strike her between the eyes. She looked at me with an expression of simultaneous disbelief and disappearance. The phrase seemed to be taking her deeply and evermore deeply to some place within that might make sense of it. She was still with the news when her legs began to search for the foyer. While she let the sentence roll about in her mind, her feet carried her almost gracefully there. I followed.

Finally she realized how wrong it sounded.

"What do you mean!? 'Had an affair'?!"

I too was shocked at the phrase, but it came out that way from wishful thinking, I suppose. Perhaps if Mrs. Benedict thought of her daughter as an adult when it had happened, she might be led to the truth gradually.

"That is incest, Doctor!" she announced to the room in general.

I nodded. "Apparently, he had been abusing her for a number of years."

She looked up. "No. Not while we were married."

112

I nodded again.

"That's not possible."

I could say nothing.

"My husband was a nothing, Dr. Kaminer! A spineless gnat! He inherited everything and created nothing. He was too insignificant to do anything that awful!"

"Your daughter loved him, Mrs. Benedict. He took advantage of that. The psychological profile of abusive fathers is frequently that of the passive human being."

"But it's not possible. I would have known. I mean, you don't keep something like that a secret."

"You do, Mrs. Benedict. You keep something like that very much a secret."

"Well. . . ." She paused.

The pause lengthened.

"Well. . . ." She paused again. "And now the police know?"

"I'm afraid so."

"Why should *they* know?"

"Someone told them. Apparently it is a big rumor in some circles."

"A big rumor!"

She sat down in a nearby hallway chair.

She seemed to be simultaneously looking for some answer in the room and for some secret hiding place within herself.

"I've done so well, Doctor," she said as the tears began to form. "I've been in AA for over two years—though I've had my slips now and then, you know? I kept with it, though. I knew drinking was a kind of slavery and at times, I feel free—certainly freer than I was before—but this, this. . . ." She couldn't find the words. "This filth!" You could almost feel it on her hands and face.

"How can I keep my head above water, stay sober, keep myself going this way when I won't even be able to hold my head up? The shame! Can you imagine what the shame will be when I drive into Ridgefield or just answer the door?"

"Mrs. Benedict—"

"I just want to give up, you know?"

"Mrs. Benedict," I said, "listen to me. Only the police have been given this information. There is no reason for it to become common gossip."

I grew quite firm with her when I saw her avoiding my eyes.

"They can't press charges or even consider an indictment without a grand jury investigation. They're not even close to that now. And if there is one shred of doubt about these rumors or anything to do with your husband killing his own daughter, the entire affair must be dropped. They cannot possibly prosecute. In that case, what's left is a few people who know—"

"But you said it was a big rumor!"

"Do you know anyone at Zion Hospital?"

She thought for a moment, then shook her head. "Where is that?"

"In Manhattan."

She sat still, then shook her head again, this time with great certainty. "No one."

114

"Do you know any doctors, physicians, or surgeons around here that practice there?"

"Why?" she asked.

"Apparently that is where the rumors began. At Zion."

Again she thought through my question. "No," she said, hesitantly at first, and then with greater assurance. "No, the doctors I know around here practice here."

"Jewish doctors?"

"Dr. Berman. He's a gynecologist. Works at the clinic here. I see him when Dr. Melrose is on vacation."

"Could he work at Zion?"

"I don't know. But he wouldn't say a thing, Doctor. He kept my alcoholism a secret for years. No, if I can trust my instincts at all, I believe he wouldn't say if he knew, and I'm quite certain if he knew anything he would have asked me to verify it. He's a superlative human being."

"You know, your former son-in-law is not too bad either. I only say that because you both may need some comforting in the next few weeks and I'd hate to have to do that all by myself."

"I should call Dr. Brockman, shouldn't I?"

"It wouldn't be a bad idea."

"That's what I'll do."

"I'm going to see her this afternoon, and I'll mention that we spoke and tell her what the police are up to."

"Thank you, Doctor. I'll call her after my meeting with them. I'll have to tell them that we spoke and that you were the first to tell my about these rumors."

"Of course, for your own sanity you must tell the truth in these situations. It's the only alternative."

115

We paused, standing in the hall a moment. She seemed frozen in thought, and then turned to me. "Goodbye, Doctor."

XXI

BEFORE I MET WITH MARION, I had the very strong instinct to call Mr. Benedict myself. I knew his name was George, that he was a member of the New York Athletic Club—Charles had mentioned feeling quite uncomfortable at their first lunch together—had no known profession to speak of, and generally spent most of his time gardening. I had also heard that his apartment in New York apparently had a balcony greenhouse that was the envy of Manhattan. I called the New York Athletic Club to leave a message but they told me that it wasn't the club's policy to leave messages for nonresiding members. I decided that when I spoke to Mrs. Benedict again I would ask for her ex-husband's address.

I skipped my lunch, which I occasionally do for my waistline. It is amazing how vanity increases in direct proportion to the fading of any evidence justifying that sin in the first place. I was quite unselfconsciously accepting in my youth of whatever gifts God gave me. Now, with their quaint deterioration, I had grown whiningly nostalgic about my former appearance. I hate people who complain about old age, but I now find myself

uncontrollably uttering the worst of clichés, i.e., "You
must forgive an old man"—which is particularly charming with younger ladies in search of a father figure but
utterly embarrassing to me. It is not forgiveness I seek. It
is the rampant advances of a heated tigress. No matter
that her needs might be entirely beyond my capacity to
appease. I say "might" because sex, for me, is based on
fantasy and there could be nothing more fantastic than
the thought of near-death ecstasy from assailing an entire
sorority house of lustful felines.

But I digress. As I was saying, after skipping my lunch,
I held to this fast by entering the progress of my investigation into a computer planner. It is an ingeniously designed project organizer that allows as freewheeling a
stream of consciousness as you might desire. If you remember to sort your thoughts by number, to know when
one ends and the other begins, then you have the almost
limitless freedom to redistribute them in any order or
any category. After doing that you may organize them
chronologically by attaching dates to either their occur-
rences or their possible terminations. Thus you have a
calendar of very precise dates and times to inspire your
concentration. Once into such pursuit, once caught in the
thrill of this hunt which frequently blossoms into some of
my best short stories, the thought of food vanishes entirely. I need my coffee, however. God bless the man who
accidentally dropped a coffee bean into his hot water. I'll
venture to say that the substance is probably responsible
for ninety percent of the literary output of the twentieth
century. Alcohol, particularly among American novelists,

has been highly overrated for its influence. Coffee is the brew and the facilitator for most of our greatest literary achievements.

On the main calendar of events we had the following ingredients:

Charles and Charlotte Manes were married on August 5, 1978. She was twenty-five and he was nineteen. So much for Marion's voyeur theory of Charles since, as an expert in the field, I find voyeurism not even diagnosable until the mid-twenties. Up until then, it is education. Their marriage, according to Charles, was prompted by a pregnancy which Charlotte miscarried six months later. I assume Charlotte must have discussed this event with Dr. Marion Brockman as a significant point in her adult life, or maybe she never mentioned the fact at all, which would have proved even more alarming.

To open this discussion with Marion I decided to bring my calendar of such important dates to my afternoon appointment with her. It would ostensibly bring a businesslike tone to what for me hopefully might prove a romantic encounter.

Her office was in a simple brownstone just off Central Park West. She herself lived around the corner in one of the nicer apartment buildings lining that extraordinary boulevard. Death, delirium, just all sorts of mayhem mingle on Central Park West with the holiday vision of fireworks erupting from the trees on the Fourth of July and blissfully silent blankets of snow in mid-February. It was a street of terminal contrasts. Marion said she found it bracing and a good reminder of the state of the world.

119

"The hope," she said, "if there is any hope for us, is right here where everything happens all at once." She shared my own enthusiasm for the thrilling disaster of Manhattan. We had exchanged lurid exclamations of tribute to the city's insanities while engaged in a rainbow of sexual postures during our unforgettable rendezvous from way too long ago. It was these images as well as a bottle of my favorite French table wine—Château Simard '85—which accompanied me as I rang her bell on West Sixty-fifth.

There was no voice on the intercom; the buzzer just rang me in.

Her office was on the first floor in the back. You walked by the stairs and encountered the kind of door you see only on the best renovations in this city: wood, a gloriously warm wood, with a glistening brass knocker on it. The door opened before I had a chance to touch it.

"Come in," she said rather too efficiently.

"Hmmmm," I murmured to myself before following her down the hallway.

We reached her office and it was apparent she wished me to take the hallowed seat of her ever-so-lucky patients. I decided to prolong the moment with my friendly offering.

"Gift-bearing Greeks are no match for wine-smuggling Southerners," I said as I offered her the bottle.

"Thank you," she said coldly.

I placed the bottle on her desk and then perused the adornments of her office. I was not, if I could help it, ever going to sit in the seat of her supplicants.

"Hmmm," I murmured again as I saw the mother-and-child art and bric-a-brac. I looked at her as if I knew that she knew that I knew how impressively manipulative all these maternal curios were.

"Have a seat," she suggested while seating herself.

"In your patients' chair? No, Marion. I will be reprimanded as a friend and colleague but I refuse to endure your free counseling. The sight of your professional mask, the horror of having to endure any patronizing demeanor after all we've shared—"

At that phrase she gave me one of her most effectively scoffing glances. I, however, pressed on.

"It would enrage me. I will behave with appropriate contrition if you just avoid swinging your saddle up on some righteously high horse."

She rose. "Perhaps a walk in the park then."

"Fine," I agreed with warm relief. "A splendid idea."

And, indeed, it was, for the park was a splendor. Autumn in New York has been slightly shortchanged by that song's prejudice for canyons of steel and shimmering clouds, entirely overlooking what is greatest about our fall season: the forests of Central Park swaying in their autumnal dance beneath the concrete and glass of this city's great cliffs. And if, while absorbing such perfection, you happen to be strolling next to a being whose very breath drives you to tears from the sheer beauty of its source, well, I don't mind telling you that heaven can wait. I've found much too much salvation right here on Earth.

Marion must have noticed my adoring glances, and

she began her first foray into my more annoying character traits.

"J.C., you mustn't pour that romantic glue all over me. I intend to be serious with you, and these loving looks will not distract me. I am worried and concerned about your health and common sense. That young man was a gentleman the other night. He might not have been. He could have taken exception to your attitude and made life quite miserable for you."

I wondered if the preceding were a fear or Marion's wishful thinking. Two men battling over a woman's favor has never put either man into any woman's true disfavor. And if she really was offended, why break a therapist's sacred rule to never offer advice when it's not asked for and certainly when it's not paid for?

"Why have you asked to see me, Marion?"

She looked quite startled at the question.

I spoke before she had a chance to respond: "Hell is paved with good intentions and your initial excuse is too pregnant with them for me to take it seriously. In the past five weeks, after a period of the past five years during which we have neither spoken, seen, nor communicated with each other in any way, we have seen or spoken to each other at least five times. Twice at my initiation and three at yours. Right now you have me outnumbered. And the truth is, I adore you. I lust for you. I have missed you quite often in the past five years, and after every time I see you I ask myself how I could have been so stupid as to let you slip through my fingers."

By now Marion refused to even look at me.

"Now I'm going to be perfectly frank with you. I ache with longing for you. I never had a better time in my life than the fifty-two hours I spent with you and I'm just too old and world-weary to play patty-cake with someone who has provoked and encouraged me to be as nakedly honest as I have ever been with anyone. I want to take you home right now, abandon myself to every possible fantasy I might come to, and inspire in you a similar frenzy."

Still she would not look at me.

"Now before we part ways, you have to quit teasing me. Actually, you have to quit calling me. And dangling that young buck in front of me was shameless. Leaving that pathetic little message on my tape was patently obvious. You love me. That was clear a long time ago and how you could remain so oblivious to your own emotional life is beyond me. Either we pick up where we left off or I just don't want to see you, ever."

She still said nothing and was even more uncommunicative than before. By now looking down at her feet and almost shuffling in a schoolgirl daze.

I decided to leave her there. I had walked about fifteen steps when I heard, "J.C.?"

There truly are times when one's own life becomes a Hollywood movie. The orchestral strings didn't rise all at once in that moment. No, I heard an oboe, a lovely and plaintive English horn with the sound of crackling chestnuts and the smell of burning leaves to it. Then as I refused to move in her direction, Marion began to walk toward me. It was then the violas began their achingly

123

sweet air. And as she approached me looking more beautiful than ever, the violins made their entrance quite subtly, and the harp, so mystically imposing when used sparingly, drew the entire ensemble together and lifted me into an utter ecstasy of expectation, all of which came true when she silently placed her perfect lips upon mine and kissed me with such a combination of purity and need that it fairly twisted my mind.

We strolled hand in hand, quite as comfortably as an old married couple, to the lobby of the Plaza Hotel where we checked into the exact room in which we had so effusively consummated our love five years before. I was a little vague as to its precise number but Marion's voice rang as clearly as I'd ever heard it.

"Room twelve-fifteen," she said with thrilling simplicity.

XXII

"YOU'RE SEEIN' HER AGAIN," SAID Mother as she ran water into a vase for the flowers I'd brought her.

After a nervous pause, I offered her an evasion that embarrassed even me.

"Seeing who?"

Mother gave me a look that hurled me back to the third grade. At eight years of age, I had involuntarily kissed a girl, Miriam Manley, who had been seated next to me in the crafts section of our local grade school. I say involuntarily because I don't ever remember planning the attack. It just happened. Miriam was skinny and awkward, but freckled and graced with the most exquisitely delicate features. Even then I seemed to know my "type." At any rate, I just threw my childish body across the aisle and laid a firm one right on her nervously thin but exciting lips.

With a gasp she stood from her school desk and wiped my kiss harshly from her mouth with a vengeance that proved most depressing in retrospect. After profoundly changing the style of all my future seductions, Miriam marched firmly to the front of the class, out the door, and directly to the principal's office.

A full three weeks later my mother found me weeping under the old willow tree out back and drew from me a most pitiable confession about how painful Miriam Manley's rejection had been: "She looked ugly, Mama. I thought she was so pretty, but when she looked at me and wiped my kiss from her lips? She looked like a witch." To which Mother replied, "That is how she will look to her husband, J.C. This is a blessing in disguise, son."

"She ratted on me, Mama!"

That's when Mother May gave me "the look," the one that prompted my recall of this incident.

"Where, may I ask, did you hear such a word?"

After shuffling my feet a bit I confessed questioningly: "Jimmy Cagney?"

"Yes, I know who he is. Did he teach you that?"

"No, Bobby Martin did. He'd been to the movies with his older brother John and that's what he said in the show."

"Bobby said that?"

"No, Jimmy Cagney said it!"

"How was John Martin allowed to take his younger brother to such a movie?"

"He told his mama that it was a Doris Day movie. And it was!" I hastened to add.

It was this vision of my childhood evasions that swept over me as Mother continued to stare through her much older but no less intensely widened eyes.

126

"Who do you think I mean?" she said with mild ferocity.

"Marion?"

"Yes," she punctuated with a period as her eyes returned to the arranging of my now increasingly modest bouquet. "Dr. Brockman."

She said the word "Doctor" as if the vision of two physicians coupling were an act against nature.

"How did you know I was seeing her?"

"The last time you brought me flowers was five years ago. Within three hours of your arrival you confessed your obsession with Ms. Brockman and asked my advice. I suggested that you consider marriage, to which you chose to embarrass yourself by reminding me of the obvious."

Mother had never been married.

Never.

After a resentful few seconds I repeated my offense: "I still don't see the difference between your decisions and mine. I abhor marriage and I know a great deal more about it than you."

I had been married.

Twice.

My first foray was in my second year of college, as a result of which my junior year was spent paying my mother back for the legal fees it took to discount the marital credits of my sophomore year.

My second failure came in my twenty-second year while abroad on a Fulbright Scholarship to Siena. It was there I had decided Anna Beatrice Curatola was, indeed, my own path to a *vita nuova* and a true link to the muses

127

of Florence—I later learned that she had really come from Pomezia, a depressing little town just south of Rome—and from the delirious heights her caresses had brought me to I would invent my own irrefutably divine comedy. Halfway through the first act—it was a play and not a poem—my Beatrice ran off with an English actor who spoke a fluent Sicilian dialect. For some bizarre reason he reminded her of her father. Apparently it was the way he uttered obscenities that drove her absolutely crazy. Their affair had been going on for at least three months before I suspected anything. By accident I heard the Fellini film he had been working on had finished weeks before. Their explanation for trips to and from Rome soon became face-reddening. Despite my age or perhaps because of it, I adopted the surrendering despair of the poor professor in *The Blue Angel.* Not coincidentally, Anna did a wicked imitation of Marlene Dietrich.

"Federico," she would say as if the great director were her chauffeur, "was so amusing today, Giuseppe."

I left Italy within twelve hours of our annulment. Yes, she'd had a priest marry us. I had forgotten to mention my earlier marriage and so the whole thing was never official anyway. Well, not officially Catholic. I appreciated the free catechism they offered me, though. The sessions spent with the local clergy greatly improved my Italian and put me in touch with my uncle Henry's strangely decadent Catholicism.

"He could sin in the most holy way," my mother once said.

My own opinion is that Italy is so profoundly carnal

an experience that God instantly offers dispensation chits to any young tourist. With that in mind I boarded an Alitalia return flight to New York, quite peacefully resigned to perpetual bachelorhood and an artfully prolonged life of extremely subtle dissipation. It was this last vow that Mother May seemed determined to interfere with.

"Marry the woman, J.C.," uttered Mother emphatically. "The pride of my independence does nothing to alleviate the horrible specter of my dying alone."

"Mama!" I quickly offered to dispel her fears with the certainty of my presence at her deathbed.

"Don't 'Mama' me!" she interrupted. "The comfort you may bring me at the end will have none of the horrid intimacy I will actually need in my last hours. You and I will always remain infernally witty with each other. Marion Brockman is both fortunately and significantly younger than you."

Then with a smile, she added: "A fluid and passionate death may very well be yours just for the asking."

On that depressing note, I picked up my portable computer and left.

XXIII

AT THE TIME OF CHARLOTTE'S murder Charles was thirty-three, the symbology of which, in light of Charles' Baptist background, did not escape our perusal.

"Charles, is it possible some darkly poetic side of your subconscious has chosen this year of your Lord to plan a bizarre form of self-crucifixion?"

Charles stared at the ceiling for some time and then remarked: "I didn't know you were a Jungian, Doctor."

After my mild surprise at his increasing erudition, I confessed: "I'm not. But when all else fails I'm willing to flirt with the devil himself to solve my clients' woes."

He said nothing, so I continued.

"You have mentioned the admonitions of your prophet, Charles—"

"My Lord," he interrupted.

"Forgive my lapse in protocol."

He looked at me with a mild irritation.

"You seem actually haunted by His sayings and not in a healthy way. I recall your mentioning his words about anger."

130

"'He that is slow to anger is better than the mighty; and he that ruleth his spirit than he that taketh a city.'"

"Hmmmmm," I murmured at the ready quickness of the quote.

"What do you say to that?" he asked.

"Zen."

"What?"

"Zen," I said even more clearly.

He sat up to listen.

"A Zen master assigns his or her pupils with an impossible task. For Christ it was this admonishment about anger and lust. Moses, as was his wont, took a longer route with the Ten Commandments. Within those expectations, however, is the hoped-for destination, the golden goal, the state of mind described by Christ as the 'heaven within' and by others as Nirvana. The student struggles to do the impossible and, of course, in utter despair and rage, fails. He curses the struggle, the master, and, finally, himself for being so stupid and incapable of change. It is then, after having killed all hopes, including those he had vested in the master, that the impossible happens. In surrender the hoped-for happens. And the truth of our frailties becomes our liberation. In Christ's interpretation it is surrendering to God, 'for Whom,' as He says, 'nothing is impossible.' For the Zen master, of course, it is surrendering to the Truth."

Charles gave me a mildly uncomprehending look. Then after a very considerable pause, he said: "You mean He never expected me to be able to do that, to never feel anger or lust?"

131

"Not on your own, he didn't. So he waits for you to invite God into your life and the only invitation that ever really reaches God is unconditional surrender."

"Do you believe in God?" he asked.

I knew I had strayed too far in issues of personal faith and had, perhaps, exposed more of Kaminer than Christ, but the risk seemed worth it, considering the situation.

"What I believe is not at issue here, Charles."

He sat silently for a moment and then said, "Thank you, Doctor."

With that he got up and left, five minutes earlier than necessary.

I report this unusual occurrence because from this point on, Charles' behavior grew increasingly more atypical.

XXIV

MR. BENEDICT GREETED ME AT the door of his brown-stone in the East Sixties. He was of average height, slightly shorter than myself, and dressed in blue jeans and a paint-spattered linen shirt. He was barefoot, and though gray, appeared extremely youthful. He could easily be mistaken for an aging matinee idol. His looks alone might have driven poor Mrs. Benedict to her drink. I suspect she had been insanely jealous of anyone and everyone who had approached him with even the slightest hint of a smile. I expect his handsomeness was what led her to ignore the signs of excessive intimacy between him and their daughter. Withdrawn he might be, but that wouldn't make him any less attractive to a grown woman.

That's how I felt until I began to notice how bizarre the man really was. It was his voice, mainly. Barely a whisper. Frequently, I had to lean forward to hear him.

"Come in," he murmured with a nod.

His arms began to gesture in the way people do when words fail them or, as I prefer to put it, when their eccentricities fail words.

Finally, it came out: "This way, Dr. Kaminer. . . . I'm uh . . . well . . . as you can see. . . ."

"I beg your pardon?" I asked.

"This way."

And he walked directly through the hallway, into the kitchen, and out the back door to a small patio of sorts. There awaiting us was a remarkably well-appointed table set for lunch. Beside it was an ice bucket which held a large bottle of Italian mineral water.

After a few more helpless gestures Mr. Benedict said: "Sit, Doctor."

After looking at what appeared to be a seriously planned meal, I said: "Mr. Benedict, I hadn't intended this to be a luncheon interview, I—"

"Oh," he sighed as loudly as he could, "you just"— again another gesture—"you just eat what you want."

"Fine," I said resignedly.

"You'll have to forgive me but I'm uh. . . ."

I had hopes he might complete the sentence. It would be the first whole thought he had uttered so far, but he paused.

"Psychiatrists scare me."

That came out as clearly as if he had spent a lifetime coming to terms with it.

I think I smiled. Yes. I did. I would have. It's not the first time I've heard it.

"I understand, Mr. Benedict. I used to scare myself a while back."

"Excuse me."

He retired to the kitchen and returned with a tray of

iced teas and fruit salad accompanied by the most extra-
ordinarily fresh sourdough rolls I was ever privileged to
taste. My plate, after he placed it before me, began to
draw me in and before I knew the fruit salad on it was
half gone and I was embarrassingly attacking my third
roll. Without butter, of course. I institute these little sacri-
fices to bolster my diminishing sense of self-control.

The prefatory amenities were quickly dispatched by
the time I was into my second helping of fruit salad and
eventually we began to enter the realm of Mr. Benedict's
most treasured pastimes.

"Painting," he said. "Above all, painting."

"Where do you paint?" I asked.

"Upstairs. On the top floor. I'm there pretty much all
day."

I nodded as I perused the various stains that dotted his
rather weathered linen shirt.

"All day, every day?"

A pause, apparently for reflection. Then: "Pretty much."

"You don't go out?"

"Not anymore."

The gestures and nervous evasions had almost entirely
disappeared. Apparently I had gotten him over his fear
of my profession.

"Which psychiatrist instilled such fear and loathing in
you?"

He smiled. "Oh, no one in particular. I guess . . ." A
nervous pause. ". . . I guess I'm afraid of my own crazi-
ness."

"Ah," I rejoined, "you think yourself insane!"

"Well . . . odd. Yes, I'm very odd. I think that's why I paint. I don't feel so lonely then, so out of place."

"May I see some of your work?"

"Nope," he said simply. "I don't show it to anyone."

"Oh." I nodded. "The last of the well-kept secrets."

"Sir?" he asked with just the slightest edge to his voice.

"My uncle Henry always said that a man, any man, goes to his grave with at least one well-kept secret."

There was a long pause during which Mr. Benedict was obviously working up the courage to ask what he inevitably did ask: "What was it?"

"Hmmmm?" I questioned.

"Your uncle Henry's last secret?"

"I have no way of knowing that and I hope and pray that my own life carries a similarly opaque conclusion to it. I am proud to say that I still have an entire list of fairly well-concealed confidences that I share only with my mirror. Life will, I assume, whittle them down."

"Isn't that *your* job?"

I gave Mr. Benedict one of my more inquisitive faces. I have an assortment of questioning looks, all very well rehearsed after thirty years of sitting Buddha-like before the rambling evasions of, if not a sea, at least an occasionally rippling pond of saddened humanity.

"Whittling down other people's secrets—that's your job, isn't it?"

"Uh-huh," I agreed.

Again I saw Mr. Benedict grow gray before my unapologetic stare.

"You wanted to see me about my son-in-law."

There was surprising backbone to his reading of these words and I was relieved to think that beneath his smoke screen of neurotic mannerisms lay a survivor.

"Yes," I said boldly. "He's in grave trouble with the law over the death of your daughter, and I suspect you can shed some light on this tragic situation."

There was one of Mr. Benedict's coyer pauses, then: "You don't think he did it."

It was a sentence which pretty well indicated that Mr. Benedict himself had his own doubts.

"No, I don't."

"Neither do I."

"I'm grateful to hear you say that. Mrs. Benedict was of quite the opposite opinion."

"I know." He smiled. "She hates Charles."

"Hated."

Mr. Benedict looked at me.

"I think she might have softened her position."

Mr. Benedict looked unconvinced.

"Be that as it may," I continued, "I need information which might help me defend him."

"You're his lawyer as well?"

"No—well, you might say that every therapist, at one time or another, becomes his client's advocate. Particularly before the court of his client's own viciously prejudicial opinion."

Mr. Benedict clearly awaited further elucidation.

"Self-loathing, Mr. Benedict. Nothing is more common among the walking wounded than suicidal delusions of *eeeevillll*."

137

Yes, I stressed the word in precisely that crazily theatrical way. I wanted to see how amused Mr. Benedict might be, to what depth his sense of humor, if he had any at all, went. From the frozen look on his face, I knew he hadn't an ounce of humor about his own condition. There was what seemed to me a full two-minute silence between the two of us, during which Mr. Benedict, after looking down for some time, picked at his food, sipped at his Pellegrino, and then began to make some eye contact again.

"You know about my daughter and me, don't you?"

"Yes, Mr. Benedict, I do. And you might be surprised to hear that Mrs. Benedict knows now as well."

Tears began to form in the man's remarkably attractive eyes. I am not homosexual per se; however, I cannot help but admit to the power of beauty over me wherever it may appear, and I suppose I could have, at another time and in another country, surrendered to the darker impulses that surround any wish to pay tribute. I am also remarkably vulnerable to the yearnings of melancholy, and at this particular moment, Mr. Benedict was immersed in a sad exquisiteness worthy of Rembrandt's *Sketches of Christ.*

"Forgive me, Doctor. Despite appearances, I'm not given to crying in front of strangers. At least, not in the last ten years or so."

"You have pulled yourself together?"

"Nothing that certain, but I have weathered the storms, so to speak, and come to some peace about it."

"Then it's highly unlikely that you murdered your daughter?"

"Is that what they're saying?"

I was impressed by Mr. Benedict's evident disinterest in who any of the "they" might be.

"It's rumored. Has even reached the police department, but they have so little to go on that any indictment is weeks away."

"Charlotte must have begun to talk."

He said this without any hint of resignation. It seemed a simple observation.

"Perhaps," I said. "But I have my doubts. Your daughter, whom I met only once, seemed much too complicated to be honest and forthright about anything. Least of all her power over you."

Mr. Benedict looked at me as if my last words had invaded a corner he thought sacred. After a brief flash of anger, he looked down resignedly and confessed.

"Yes, I had no will of my own. I knew it was wrong. Terribly, terribly wrong. I would shake my head at the very moment of contact."

He then looked at me to see how shocked I'd be.

"But then she would . . ."

He couldn't complete the sentence.

I, on the other hand, was desperate to hear the "she woulds" and "she coulds" of it. Incest is a land so few experience that any glimpse of it is like a car accident. One cannot bear to watch, but one cannot look away.

"No," he shook his head. "No. I cannot blame her. It

wasn't sex with her, it was power, and what child doesn't want to have complete power over their own parents?"

"None living that I know," I encouraged.

"I taught her every filthy word I knew. And coming from her sweet little mouth it was . . ."

He rose as if to breathe, as if the memories had somehow stopped his lungs and the weight of his melancholy and lust would swallow him up right there before my eyes.

"If you'll excuse me, Doctor, I must end this little interview. It is not doing me one bit of good. It is, in fact, dragging me back to a time I thought I had erased. Do you understand?"

I nodded.

"Do you understand well enough to leave my home now and never come back?"

After a long look at him, I said: "Yes."

At the front door I stopped and made him an offer: "If, however, you need me to help you in any way, to testify as to the highly unlikely possibility of your killing your own daughter, if you need any assistance in that regard at all, I would be most willing to oblige."

"Thank you, Doctor."

XXV

"You didn't!!" she screamed.

"I did."

"Lunch?! With that disgusting—"

"Whoa," I said. "Wait a minute, Marion."

"There's no wait-a-minute about it, J.C. The man's beneath whatever is beneath contempt."

I watched her parade about the room in her altogether. She had been nestled quite dreamily in the crook of my naked arm, and within seconds she was there in the middle of my bedroom modeling her birthday suit to the accompaniment of a most extravagant tirade.

"The Marquis de Sade had the distinctly moral high ground of his honesty! He buried *his* soul and anything approaching redemption in a kind of protective audacity."

I was noticing how much she was beginning to sound like me.

"Uh-huh." I nodded in approval at the mildly rosy rhetoric.

"But Benedict?! He had no soul at all! No courage, no concern, no truth, no love, not even the slightest shred of sensitivity about what he was doing to Charlotte. I may be willing to accept her as a seductress all her life, but that creep of a father. . . ."

I was disappointed at that particular choice of words. Mundane, guttural, and highly unimaginative.

I urged her on: "Crepuscular lichen!!"

"What?"

"Parasite! Leeching, scabracious pustule!!"

She had stopped in smiling consternation at my interruptions.

"Smegmatic toe-jam, drippin' from the crotch of Beelzebub himself!! A disease conceived amidst the short hairs that surround the anus, the blister that lies just beneath the tail root of the demon."

She gave me an "are-you-finished" look, then wandered a bit less furiously about the room in a kind of thoroughbred cooling-off ritual.

Finally she simply repeated the dreaded thought: "You had lunch with him."

Nodding, I said: "Yes, broke bread with the devil himself and found him to be almost as charming as legend would have it but in a way entirely unexpected. His shyness—"

At this Marion scoffed and did her little "ruffled" dance, her figurative feathers all preened and high in dudgeon, ending in a small but intensely appealing crossing of the arms over her moderately sized but perfectly shaped breasts.

I rose to try and calm her but the movement only made her turn away.

"I mean it, Marion. He is still in a great deal of pain."

"Oh, I'll bet he is. All weepy and soft-spoken."

"Yes."

"And you fell for it."

"Yes, I did. There is a very hypnotic agony about him. A kind of Hamlet with silver hair but sporting a simpler, more American intelligence. I would love to loose you on him and see how grand your indignation remains in the face of his obvious suffering."

"Oh, J.C.," she scoffed, "you *love* suffering. You *love* confusing victims and victimizers."

"And which are you, my love, so utterly at the mercy of my raving insensitivity? Victim or victimizer? What must I do to convince you of your own, deliciously ruthless power over me?"

By then I was kneeling before her, my face nestled against her lusciously soft abdomen.

I felt her hands touching my hair with a much gentler inclination, something almost motherly despite the fact that my own urgings had an entirely different flow to them.

"J.C., the man's own analyst left him in disgust. How could you even think of meeting with him, let alone offering sympathy?"

I hadn't really heard this at first, so involved with Em's stomach I was.

"Em, have you been working out? Your tummy has grown slightly too firm for my touch."

She smacked me lightly on the head and walked into the bathroom.

There I was, kneeling in the middle of my own bedroom, quite naked and still staring at the retreating derrière of my beloved when it struck me what she'd said.

"His own *analyst?!*"

She didn't answer from the bathroom. I followed her in.

"What do you mean, he was left by his own analyst?"

"Martin Lodge."

The name rang a distant bell somewhere in my professional-journals file. I ran the sound of it around some of the more hollow spaces of my memory and came up with some distant image of a seminar or benefit.

"Lodge. From the Institute?"

"No. *Dr.* Lodge. A late bloomer. Didn't go analytic until his late thirties."

By now Em was flossing her teeth, a thing she did with infuriating frequency. Her smile was, I must admit, blinding, but her attachment to that horrid little plastic dispenser was borderline. She kept one in her handbag and others in the random pocket or two.

She spoke through the sometimes grotesque effects of her dental ministrations.

"Charlotte mentioned him in passing."

"He was her father's therapist?"

"Years before. Many years before."

"How many years?"

"Fifteen, at least. He had been treating Benedict when the horrid man confessed to molesting his daughter."

"And Lodge left him?!"

"I think he did the right thing. Apparently it came as such a surprise he was embarrassed at his own lack of

144

knowledge about a client's self-destructive behavior. Thought he'd been enabling him in some way, so he stopped treatment altogether."

"How do you know all of this?"

Em paused in one of her coyer poses and waited, as if determining whether or not to free some sort of secret.

"I wanted to know what ended her relationship with her father. She said Dr. Lodge. From that point on, her father wouldn't see her. They'd only talk on the phone and usually when she called."

"Where does he work out of?"

"Dr. Lodge?"

"Which hospital?"

"Kennedy."

"Not Zion?"

"Hardly."

I wasn't sure what she meant by that.

"You have to be Jewish to understand, J.C."

"He's prejudiced?"

She shook her head and then added: "Self-loathing."

XXVI

I FOUND DR. LODGE'S NUMBER in the phone book. I wasn't particularly eager to let Marion know how far I might pursue her revelations. Her reaction to my meeting with Mr. Benedict quite ended my streak of complete and utter honesty. This, if nothing else, has convinced me that marriage cannot survive the truth.

"May I ask who's calling?" said the receptionist.

"Kaminer. Dr. J. C. Kaminer."

"Hold, please."

The voice was pleasant but peremptory.

After a few seconds: "Yes?"

"Dr. Lodge?"

"Yes?"

"I'm not sure if you remember me."

"Of course I remember you. Who wouldn't?"

"Well, in all honesty, I can't remember if it was a convention or a benefit."

"It was an opening."

"Really?"

"Yes. Barnard Reckling's first."

"Reckling?"

"Nineteen ninety-one. The Stimmer Galleries. On Fifty-seventh."

"Oh!"

Oh, I remembered achingly. I had buried any memory of the event. What hung on the wall was so disastrous I became embarrassed for its creator, who happened to be racing eagerly about the room soliciting the most shameless forms of flattery. By the time he had approached me for an appraisal I was well into my fifth glass of wine and quite unable to summon up even the slimmest form of civility. I could see him looking at me looking at the paintings.

"Mr. Kaminer?"

"*Doctor* Kaminer," I corrected.

"Forgive me. Is it true that your uncle was the great Henry Albright Kaminer?"

I waited in my mild stupor for some charitably disposed common sense to possess me, to lead me still polite, if a bit wobbly, to the door and out to the relatively fresher air of Fifty-seventh Street. Pollution, even the tenaciously invasive Manhattan brand, is a much more enlivening brew than hypocrisy. Unfortunately, I, when well oiled, am not in the habit of retreat.

"He still is," I replied.

"My God," exclaimed the waterfly, "he's still alive?"

"No, but death has not altered our bloodlines one eeney-teeney-weeney little bit."

The "eeney" was excessive, I know, two syllables quite

147

beyond the pale of normal confrontation, but staring into this puckering sycophant's bright and dizzy little eyes just drew up all of my mimetic venom.

After a startled pause, the fool continued: "I think he is the second greatest art critic of the twentieth century."

"And the first?"

"Bernard Berenson."

He said this as if it were so self-evident only children would mistake the obvious.

"Bernard Berenson was *never* a critic of the twentieth century."

"I beg your pardon—" the upstart exclaimed.

I went on, however: "I doubt if a painting younger than Methuselah himself ever reached the man's consciousness, let alone his acknowledgment."

"Oh," he fumbled, "I misunderstood you."

"Don't be modest, young man. Judging from your work you have misunderstood the Universe, not to mention the simple, humble confines of every breath you've taken."

"Uh," he began.

"The line of your creations," I continued, pointing to the nearest without looking, since the one I faced on the other wall was simply a mirror reflection of its own stupidity and all the others just a continuing repetition of this man's one discovery in life—that red and blue sometimes go together—"this unremitting repetition of your ineptitude?! The lifeless configuration of your markings—I hesitate to call them designs since that would admit of some conscious understanding, some craft-bearing commitment to the natural order of things, some talent—the overall, boring chaos (and *that* contradiction in terms may be your only achievement so far), the entire display?"

At this point I was briefly at a loss for not only words but enthusiasm since the object of my onslaught was so unworthy of even my scorn, in light of this proof of my penchant for overkill, that I simply exclaimed: "Lord, show me some fresh air before I pass out from the lack of stimulation!"

At that point I ambled (with remarkable abandon for the state I was in—I even recall tossing off a few quick dance steps) toward the door. There, near its opening, stood Dr. Lodge.

"Bravo," he applauded quietly. "Mr. Reckling could hardly reckon with you."

I was not overwhelmed with this pun and almost turned my arsenal on him, but something about his genuine warmth, the effortless way his smile played across his face, stopped and actually relaxed me. As entertaining as an insulting tirade might appear, it does drain its author with the instant hangover, the secret guilt that accompanies all preemptive judgment. Yes, if I have a flaw it is an Old Testament urge toward accusation. I'm sure Mr. Reckling's supercilious character must have had some redeeming social value to it despite all evidence to the contrary. I was in no condition, however, to undertake the thorough investigation needed to find it.

149

"Dr. Lodge," said the man at the door. "A pleasure to meet you."

"Kaminer," I responded with mild politeness. "J. C. Kaminer."

"*Doctor* Kaminer," he underlined.

"Not today," I said with slight embarrassment. "Not today."

Then, if I remember correctly, I exited.

Now on the phone to this same man, I endeavored to avoid any review of my little Waterloo. "Dr. Lodge," I began politely, "I would like to meet with you regarding the death of Charlotte Benedict. As I understand it, you were Mr. Benedict's therapist for some time."

There was a pause at the end of the line.

"Dr. Lodge?"

"What is your connection to the Benedicts?"

"Charles Manes is a patient of mine."

Another pause, even longer this time, during which I could almost hear the doctor's synapses firing in rapid computation over the possible implications. "Where would you like to meet?"

"Anywhere and anytime you please, Doctor."

The Manhattan Athletic Club is one of the last bastions of gentile male prejudice left in the city. Its racism has fallen or, to put it more accurately, been obscured more by the forces of a fading economy than any other, possibly humane impulse. Now, the relatively recent Jewish and black membership speak proudly of its openness while their real reason for joining is to show that they are,

indeed, the exception. At the luncheon I shared with Dr.
Lodge, there was no one even appreciably "ethnic" in the
entire dining room. I now understood Marion's reference
to the doctor's self-loathing. I assumed that both the
name and the puckish features were an almost felonious
misrepresentation of what Nature had intended. I was
left, however, with the unanswerable question of what
exactly God *had* intended.

"It's a pleasure to meet you at last, Doctor, in quieter
circumstances than our last meeting."

He spoke these words with the slightly frozen-jawed
gentility of many well-to-do Ivy alumni.

"Yale?" I asked.

He smiled almost apologetically. "No, Columbia."

"You're from Manhattan?"

"Yes," he said simply, as if to close the subject.

"You sound ashamed of that fact."

"Do I?"

"I would have risked not just purgatory but some
milder corner of hell to have lived here my entire life."

"But then you wouldn't be you, would you?" he murmured almost enviously.

Yes, thought I as I sipped the mediocre beginnings of
my gazpacho, I do have a problem child before me. A
pause continued while our separate evaluations of each
other silently danced between the arrival of the waiter to
pour more water and Dr. Lodge's introduction to what
proved an even more impressive dance of evasions.

"Dr. Kaminer," he began, "I've researched your back-

ground a bit since we spoke on the phone—I'm sure
you've done a bit of the same—and I've read and heard
of some startling opinions."

He paused, expecting, I suppose, some reaction from
me. My silence didn't entirely unnerve him, but the smile
that blossomed on his face didn't appear to be the fruit of
any pleasure.

"*Your* opinions. Of psychiatry."

Again I offered him no solace.

"If you harbor such contempt for psychiatry, why do
you even practice?"

I thought if I ate through my response it might give Dr.
Lodge a more effective sense of my flippancy. So the following struggled through mouthfuls of soup, bread, water, and an occasional gesture to the waiter for my salad.

"Psychiatry pays for my lunches, Dr. Lodge. And my
concert tickets. My first-class accommodations to and
from Europe, where I spend extravagant amounts of
money devouring delicacies so far superior to the ones
I'm savoring now that it would be impolite of me to risk
further comparison. I live on the expensive side of Fifth
Avenue, enjoy the companionship of equally spoiled
dilettantes such as myself, present company not ex-
cluded, and by and large, have discovered that in addition to soaking the rich for their mostly imagined wars
with inner demons, I myself have grown wealthy and
mistakenly respected because I have the title 'M.D.' after
my name. Add up the pros and cons, the victories and
defeats of the entire medical profession and, though not
placing us completely in the minus column, it does re-

duce the more arrogant and prideful in our profession to the relative importance of New York public school custodians who, as I understand it, are equally overpaid for their sloth."

After a slight pause, the doctor offered: "Did you come here to interview me or insult me?"

"I may be wrong," I said as I continued my feast, "but I do believe you asked me a question. To which I replied as thoroughly as I could without spoiling this meal with a lecture."

"So you live comfortably with your self-loathing?"

"Well," I replied, "I certainly haven't disguised it."

I tried to personalize my statement by looking directly into his eyes.

"No," he said, either ignoring or totally unaware of my inferences, "Dr. Kaminer, you certainly haven't done that. You pride yourself on being frank, that's obvious."

"No, I was trying to reveal," said I through the crackling of my bread stick, "that I don't pride myself on much of anything. I am one of the lucky few on whom God has chosen to lavish material blessings. I am returning the favor by enjoying each of them as profoundly as possible."

"You are a very intimidating man. But you know that, don't you?"

"Yes, Doctor, I do."

I waited to see what treasures my intimidating manner might elicit, but Dr. Lodge fell to his own food and it was up to me to continue the interview.

"You were Mr. Benedict's therapist for some time, is that correct, Doctor?"

153

"Yes," he said. "Almost ten years."

"As I understand it, you ended sessions upon discovering that he was sexually molesting his daughter."

After a slight and disconcerted pause, he said: "Yes, but how did you know that?"

I wasn't sure whether telling him Marion Brockman's name would be sufficient or simply complicate matters further.

"Your client, Charles Manes?"

"No. Unfortunately, things are more complicated than any of us would want them to be."

I thought I had opened up enough subject matter to let the discussion simmer in silence.

"Yes, Doctor, but isn't that what we're here for? Hasn't life—or God, as you might prefer—handed us so many complexities that we can't possibly confront them alone? I've always fancied therapy as the new confessional."

He paused as if I should be intrigued by the novelty of such a metaphor.

I wasn't.

"In ages before," he continued, "and most profoundly in the Dark Ages, the Church provided the only soul food available to the masses. That relationship between priest and sinner, though bound in immense superstition and dogma, did provide a place for intimacy. Not even wives heard what the Father Confessor had heard. In the same way, we in the twentieth century are enacting a rite that has existed for hundreds of years. Freud didn't invent psychic healing. He simply replaced the priest with a more compassionate ear."

"Are you a Catholic, Doctor?" I asked, almost blushing with the audacity of my deception.

He actually smiled with satisfaction, as if somehow his whole costume and disguise had convinced me.

"No," he said almost smugly.

"Protestant?"

"No. I imagine you'd have to describe me as a lapsed theist."

"Hmmmmmmmm," I intoned in my most appreciative expression of shock at the impressive duplicity of sighted blind men.

"You believed in God at one time?" I asked.

"No. My parents led me to believe I did."

He wisely returned to his food at the first unique turn of phrase he had made so far.

"What do you think," I said to move things along, "Mr. Benedict led his *daughter* to believe?"

"About God? I don't know. As to the messier things of life, I think he just made them messier."

"Do you think *he* might have killed Charlotte?"

"No."

He said this so clearly and simply that my estimate of him rose appreciably.

"I've met the man," I said, "and I agree with you entirely."

"Did he mention me?"

"No."

"Did Charley ever mention me?"

"Mr. Benedict's daughter?" I asked, quite surprised by Dr. Lodge's use of her favorite diminutive.

155

"Yes."

"No," I said. "Did you know her at all?"

"We had an affair."

I was shocked, a reaction that is not one of my more common experiences, and I'm still not sure why this took me so by surprise but I had just never made such a connection. Even now it seems a bit outlandish.

"It was long after I had terminated Mr. Benedict's therapy," he said. "Another ten years, to be exact. Charley had come to me for help."

"As a psychiatrist?"

"Yes. Of course, I immediately explained to her the unfortunate cross connections with her father made it impossible."

Here the doctor paused and took a rather deep breath. He seemed to be exhaling an almost audible thought: that had he followed his own good advice he might not be feeling the discomfort he was about to endure in the next few minutes of his confession.

"I've analyzed and analyzed this mistake of mine from every possible angle and I keep coming up with self-destruction. Mine. Not hers."

He looked briefly up at me and continued: "I'm not sure why I'm telling you all of this. You are a therapist, however, and perhaps might be of some assistance in this. I know you are preoccupied with Charles Manes' indictment at the moment. That, however, will pass eventually and the simple matter of getting on with the everyday will return. I'm not suicidal over my indiscretions with Charley, never have been, but I do have a long list of unanswered questions about why I might have fallen in the way I did. Why I risked everything like that for someone so obviously self-destructive. And, if you'll forgive my saying it, so evil. Not even the Holocaust had me entirely convinced of the devil's existence, but after a year's involvement with Charlotte Manes I'm certain that some people are just possessed by darkness."

He paused again without looking up. Then he continued: "Something at the center of her, something like an abyss, the kind of thing you drop pebbles into or shout at and get nothing back except, perhaps, memories of your own worst nightmares, the kind you see becoming real around a woman like Charley."

"Nightmares?" I interrupted.

"Yes. Of blackmail, mainly. Oh, she never asked for money. Didn't have to. It was evidence of love and loyalty she demanded. Displays of affection in places so dangerously exposed I became unable to sleep at night for fear the phone would ring with some neighbor's gossip about my infidelity. We even crossed paths socially once, and with our respective spouses looking on, Charlotte flirted outrageously with me. Little did I know that by then her husband had been cuckolded more times than he'd reached the free throw line."

The obvious pain on Dr. Lodge's face made smiling at his comparison impossible.

"Mr. Manes just seemed to stare blindly through the entire introduction. My wife, Miriam, she wouldn't be appeased in her suspicions until I lied to her that Charlotte had been hospitalized for chronic indecent expo-

157

sure. It wasn't true. Charlotte only exposed herself if you did. Besides, no one in that family by then cared enough for Charlotte to have her hospitalized for anything. Except for an abortion. I remember that very well. No one was quite sure who the father was."

"Was this possibly *your* child?" I asked in such a mesmerized tone that I felt I'd lost all professional objectivity and had begun to listen to this story as if it were being told in the theater by a very skilled actor.

"No," said Dr. Lodge. "Our relationship hadn't begun yet. Perhaps it was the pity she inspired, the pain she conveyed at having to abort a child she really wanted, perhaps that was the final and most seductive weapon she used on me. At any rate, it wasn't long after that our affair began."

"Where?" I asked, a bit too eagerly for my own taste.

"In my office," he said.

He paused with that silent cry some people can make for a comforting interruption, for some polite question that might lift them out of their agony. True to my profession, I brought him no solace. I let him sit there in the mess he'd conjured up, hoping the pain might inspire him to further confessions.

"Despite my realization that it went against all the ethical dictates of our profession . . . despite all the arguments I presented to her . . . despite all the arguments I made inwardly, entreaties to myself to remain sensible, professional . . . despite everything, she became my patient. In no time, of course, I was under her thrall."

He looked away, clearly embarrassed, unable to meet my gaze. He took a deep swallow of his wine.

"She began to dress in a way that pleased me more. Perhaps the art work in my office and the photos of my wife and daughter gave her an indication of what might make me feel at home with her. This was something I was only aware of later, and realized how much a part of the seduction it was. At any rate, this little crocheted handkerchief she'd begun to bring to our sessions fell to the floor one day and she actually knelt down to look for it. The kneeling, I'm sure, wasn't necessary but it did bring me out of my chair and around the front of my desk. It was there that her childlike appearance and all of the memories and images that her father had left in my mind, years before, the kind of pictures he was very adept at painting invaded me. With words, mind you. I know he does watercolors but that's not the limit of his talents. He had a way of describing sex with his daughter that made it horrifyingly real and irresistible. I think I ended my sessions with him out of simple self-defense. I put it in the manner of a threat and then a punishment, that if he didn't end his disgraceful behavior I would have to terminate his therapy. I think he actually *wanted* me to go to the police. I was obliged by law to do it. I should have. But I knew I would have to testify and be consulted in a criminal investigation, in a very unsavory scandal. I just thought that if I dropped him, never treated him again, that it would all go away. But when his daughter, the very object of his lust, the very participant in the incredible orgies that he had described—they were away together for days, doctor, whole vacations in a hotel room—"

There was another long pause in which Dr. Lodge seemed to be searching for some key or secret to his story. It was at this point that I squirmed uneasily in my seat at the recognition of how enjoyable this tale had become. The slow but unrelenting description of such a classic indecency as incest, such a profoundly forbidden fruit, was riveting. I don't recall ever being that captivated in a theater or concert hall. As my experience of these intimacies grew more mesmerizing I began to wonder how complicitous I was in eroticizing the destruction of any child's normal ties to his or her community. The only similar experience I'd had was in reading Anaïs Nin's description of her love affair with her father in 1933. Quite boldly, candidly, and unapologetically, the French/American diarist recorded in detail the repeated assignations she shared with Joaquin Nin, the Spanish musician and artist. There even came a point where Ms. Nin had initiated the sex herself. From that point on her notes are quite shameless, not only in the description of her father but of the occasional lust she felt for him while alone. Not coincidentally, Miss Nin proved not only literal in her sexual pursuit of father figures but relentlessly symbolic as well. Not one, but both of her analysts—Dr. René Felix Allendy and the famous Dr. Otto Rank—fell to the powers of this seductress.

"I wanted to know *Charlotte's* side of it, I guess," continued Dr. Lodge after a long pause. "Yes, after our affair had begun, I would ask her the memories she had. I'd say, 'Charley, what happened in Palm Beach?' And she'd tell me. Every detail. As we made love, she'd remind me of the things she'd done to her own father."

Neither Dr. Lodge nor I had eaten a single mouthful since this story began and it would have continued if the infernal waiter hadn't interrupted.

"Is there anything wrong with your lunches, gentlemen?"

Dr. Lodge looked up suddenly and covered for both of us.

"No, Stanley," he said. "Everything is fine. I'm just going over old times with an old friend."

"Would you like to have your meals reheated?"

"No," I said, tasting my omelette. "Your eggs have actually improved this way."

The waiter gave me his most heavily lidded look and left. After a suitable pause to return us to the world of Charlotte Manes, Dr. Lodge ended the tale with a simple admission.

"The affair," he said, "didn't cost me my marriage or even my reputation, but I'm not the doctor I thought I was. I'm not the man I wanted to be."

"Which of us is?" I interjected earnestly, in perfect sympathy with Dr. Lodge's growing honesty.

He looked up from the lowered gaze his thoughts had brought to his visage.

"What man," I continued, "has even the slightest shadow of the perfection his boyhood dreams demanded of him?"

161

He looked at me directly for perhaps the first time in our interview.

"I'm certain you're a great therapist. I've never described my affair with Charley in more detail than now. To anyone. So you must have the gift. I mean, a talent beyond even the legend you've built with Charles Manes."

The smile he included with the last sentence seemed to be saying that this candidness was about to end.

"Charles is about to be tried for murder, Dr. Lodge. I'd hardly call that a success story."

"If you knew Charlotte Manes you might consider his crime a civic duty."

The air filled heavily with all the provocation Dr. Lodge's remark intended.

"Those words," I said, "could make you a suspect, Doctor."

"Then I'm standing in a very long line."

I had nothing to say. When sentences begin to roll out of people's mouths that have no other intention but to provoke curiosity, I have the perverse impulse to fall into utter silence, to express not a whit of interest in either the provocation or the provocateur.

Apparently, Dr. Lodge wasn't going to continue in this direction, for he dug into his very cold entree, a veal piccata, quite heartily.

I tended seriously to my omelette, a meal I didn't consider anything to put me in Dr. Lodge's debt since I was his obligatory guest—you only sign for meals in the Manhattan Athletic Club.

"Doctor," I said, "are you as forthcoming about your background as you are about your sexual life?"

There was a very nasty pause here. I had obviously struck blood and the vampire in me hovered excitedly over Dr. Lodge's darkening looks.

"What did Dr. Brockman tell you?" he asked calmly.

I don't know why this question surprised me. I should have known after hearing of the doctor's affair with Charlotte Manes that he might also be acquainted with her last therapist, but since Marion was so frank in her opinion of Dr. Lodge's character, I had neglected to ask her about anything else. That was something she might have intended—bold news to put off any further investigation. Now I suspected that I had received this long confession from Dr. Lodge because he perhaps assumed Marion knew and had told me all about his affair with Charlotte Manes.

"Dr. Brockman told me," I began in replay, "that you had been Mr. Benedict's therapist and that you were self-loathing. Other than that? Nothing. Certainly not anything concerning an affair between you and her former client."

Dr. Lodge grew almost red with anger. He had miscalculated. He had thought this confession of his might inspire pity in me. His voice grew curt and precise.

"She called me an anti-Semitic Jew, correct?"

After taking in this change of tone, I replied: "Is she wrong?"

"I know a number of Jews who are Francophiles, An-

163

glophiles, even Germanophiles. Does that make *them* anti-Semitic?"

"It certainly wouldn't make them happy," I answered. "How can you love any nation that has a history of hating you and yours? We're sitting in a small version of one right now. Why would you ever want to share membership in this establishment? I certainly wouldn't join the General Sherman Memorial Racquet Club."

All of the doctor's bolder aura seemed to collapse like a dying dirigible. His certainty quavered and then broke onto some imaginary no-man's-land that hung between our looks. The strong-jawed clarity drooped and a slack-jawed stare replaced it until he suddenly rose.

"Excuse me, please."

I watched him leave the big room and turn left toward what I presumed to be the rest rooms.

"Hmmm," I hummed to myself.

I waited to be moved, one way or another, by this abrupt departure, but I had lost all sympathy for him. Instead I stared at my frozen omelette and called the waiter over to order a nice, tall white Lillet on the rocks with two orange twists.

"Dessert," I whispered to myself.

Dr. Lodge returned with the most painfully reddened eyes and an air of brusque propriety.

"Forgive me," he said coldly. "What were we talking about?"

"Self-loathing," I said. "We were discussing self-loathing, and if I remember correctly, it was a subject you broached originally in regard to my opinions of psychiatry."

164

"Oh, yes. Well, you can have whatever opinions you like. You don't need me to tell you that, but you might hear me out enough, just briefly enough, to learn that I would like you to mind your own business."

I gave Dr. Lodge one of my more archly surprised, who-the-hell-do-you-think-you-are looks. I felt my eyebrows reach the beginnings of my boldly receding hairline.

"Forgive me, Doctor," I replied, "but isn't that exactly the business we both are in—the I-can-never-mind-my-own-business business?"

He tried the smile now. It was one of those aren't-you-a-witty-son-of-a-bitch smiles. A thin-lipped grin that was pasted on. Above it, the deadly eyes gazed off at an eternal enemy. Clearly this relationship was by now on the other side of war. So, I thought, what the hell—I'll drop the hydrogen bomb.

"I think it's entirely possible, Doctor, that *you* killed Charlotte Manes."

Without losing a centimeter of his smile, the doctor nodded in mild surprise.

"An affair," I continued, "with one of your own clients, with the daughter of another, former client who had admitted to an incestuous relationship with her? Hmmmm. Much more embarrassing than any allegations of your being an anti-Semitic Jew."

"Dr. Kaminer, when are you going to quit responding to the agonies of a scorned applicant? Dr. Brockman herself had sought a position on the staff of my hospital and was rejected! Is she also self-loathing for wanting to practice among the gentiles?"

165

The gentiles, I thought. Hmmmm, not "gentiles" but "*the* gentiles." Rather like "*The* 21 Club" or "*The* Savoy."

"She hasn't Ivied up her diction," I responded pugnaciously, "or had her nose bobbed, doesn't dine at infamously restricted clubs, has a penchant for blisteringly frank admissions which are free of any ulterior motives—"

"Meaning what, sir?" asked the doctor.

"That little confession of yours about Charley. You knew if I hadn't already known about it I might have eventually learned it from Dr. Brockman, and wouldn't it be more profitable for you to admit it outright."

A very disturbing pause occurred during which I could hear the doctor's synapses again.

"What do you two share," he asked, "that would make Dr. Brockman break her client/patient obligations? How intimate *are* you with her?"

I lied. I hate to admit it but I lied right through my teeth and my double Lillet.

"Unfortunately, Dr. Lodge, not as intimate as I would like to be."

Actually, that was not entirely untruthful. There were many, perhaps hundreds, of possible permutations of the love act that I hadn't even begun to explore with Marion.

"I confess," I continued, "to a very one-sided admiration for Dr. Brockman. She is obviously beautiful, intelligent, frank, and forthcoming—all traits I consider to be entirely irresistible."

After a pause, Dr. Lodge said: "Then I'm surprised you didn't fall for the charms of Charley."

After a quick calculation, I replied: "Mrs. Manes was

beautiful, yes. Forthcoming to a fault. But frank? I'm not so sure. Shocking, yes. Evasive, certainly. But intelligent? Hardly on a par with Dr. Brockman."

"So Dr. Brockman is not even an admirer of yours?" Hmmmm, I thought. How deep in the lie must I go?

"I doubt," I offered beneath lowered eyes, "if I'm in any of her better graces than you, Dr. Lodge."

"No," he said, "I believe I'm the first on her hate list."

"No, Doctor, that lofty honor goes to Charlotte's father. The very mention of his name summons up not only her blood but the invective of a stevedore."

"So you *have* had an affair with her."

Uh-oh, I thought, the man's not as narcissistic as I thought.

"What makes you think that?" I asked.

"Dr. Brockman is the type of woman who could only lower herself to profanity in the presence of a lover. I was raised with women like her. My sister is almost her spitting image. When her boyfriend told me she'd said the word 'fuck' in front of him, I knew they had to be serious. They were married not six months after that. I'm now the proud uncle of two boys and a girl."

After a pause, he added: "Her husband is Catholic. I wouldn't be surprised if I suddenly read in the newspapers about your *engagement* to Dr. Brockman."

"Did you kill Charlotte Manes?" I asked.

The "smile" crept again over Dr. Lodge's face.

"If you confess to making love to Dr. Brockman," he murmured coyly, "then I'll tell you whether or not I killed Charley."

167

I thought the bargain through and found it entirely inequitable. In my heart of hearts I couldn't care less who had killed Charlotte Manes. Oh, my client was at risk, but even *he* held no match for the old Southern gallantry that Marion has always inspired in me.

"I would never," I said archly and in, if not my highest dudgeon, at least my most musical, "admit to something like that. It is demeaning to all the parties involved, including you for asking. I hold indiscretion about a loved one at least on a par with incest. You should be ashamed for asking such a question."

"But that's the business we're in—right, Doctor?"

"No, sir. Curiosity, professional or otherwise, should never interfere with the actions of common decency and self-respect."

"Then the only possible resolution for both of us," he said as he laid his napkin with finality on the table, "is silence. Waiter?"

Dr. Lodge asked briskly for the check, signed it, and left.

XXVII

THERE IS AN INN TWO hours' drive from the city, called the White Hart. It's in Salisbury, Connecticut, a town whose namesake in England contains one of the most beautiful cathedrals in the world. I make impulsive pilgrimages to this inn thinking that its location carries spiritual implications. It's foolish of me, I know, but it helps me combine a precipitous escape from Manhattan with an aura of religious retreat, thus absolving me of whatever excesses I might indulge in. Their restaurant has an occasional wine-tasting special, a splendid excuse for experimenting one's way into mild oblivion. My first evening is usually spent in this polite form of Dionysian tribute, a new white or red selection being served with each course of the meal. The next morning is spent recovering, particularly from whatever *new* wine has been served. After that, my second and, if I am blessed with such liberty, third mornings are spent giving my entire life serious consideration. In my rental car I scoot about the neighboring countryside while the more profound questions I've asked myself continue their inquisitorial dance amidst the dangling participles of my subconscious. Eventually, the entire *mishegoss*—yes, I am bilingual—or at least the overall swamp of metaphysical implications will receive some enlightenment. The insights I do arrive at, however, have a battery life of about thirty-six to forty-eight hours, during which I am utterly convinced that I have discovered the secret of life. Between all the wine and the wisdom, I receive more than my money's worth. I return to Manhattan, if not refreshed, at least convinced that the White Hart Inn is unquestionably a "deer" hotel.

It was with one of those experiences in mind that I returned there fresh on the heels of my encounter with Dr. Lodge at the Manhattan Athletic Club. I was positive after my first evening's meal in the inn that the answer to the question "Who killed Charlotte Manes?" would spring fully formed, if not from my forehead, at least from my endless forebodings. I was worried that the killer might strike again. Now, that could either exonerate my client or plunge him even more deeply into a criminal proceeding. It is at times like these one wishes bail to be a more stringent door to temporary freedom. Were Charles in jail he would at least be exculpated of all subsequent copycat crimes.

Who knows, I thought to myself as I lay on the bed of my room at the inn, I could be next. I'd been nosin' around enough to scare someone. This being my first "caper," so to speak, my maiden voyage as a sleuth, I felt somewhat at the mercy of my own imagination. Perhaps only in the movies are killers so blithely driven to kill again.

It was, however, after waking suddenly from a subsequent nap at the White Hart, a slumber induced largely by the effects of the inn's banana cream and black-bottom pie, that I saw my suspect list expanding rather than contracting. There were Charles himself, of course, and Dr. Lodge, who had leapt to the top of the list with his performance at the Manhattan Athletic Club; Charles' bodyguard, Dooby, whose eager helpfulness seemed a little strange; Charlotte's father, though I doubted his ability to kill anyone or anything but his own self-respect; and, possibly, a score of Charlotte's former lovers. Who might they be?

It might help, I thought, if I just climbed back into bed and let the myriad threads of my recent investigation swirl me about in their labyrinth, play at the roots of my curiosity until the most glaring clues rose up to my consciousness. A romantic notion of detective work, I know, but perfectly in sync with my style of life at the White Hart. Perhaps I could escape my way to a solution. So that is what I did. After filling my coffee thermos at the dining room—I carry some such thing on all of my road trips—I retired to my room, disrobed in a suitably piecemeal and relaxed fashion, propped myself up in bed with a good book, and then waited for the suspicious non sequiturs of my research to raise their neglected and resentful little heads. Only one such progeny revealed itself: abortion.

Hmmmm.

Charlotte had had an abortion. Charles knew nothing about it. Had accepted his wife's explanation: miscarriage.

171

Surely Marion would know more of this.

"Marion," I said with the phone propped against my pillowed ear and my expectations deflated by the recording tape I was obliged to speak to, "I need to know something more about Charlotte. Please call me at the White Hart Inn, Salisbury, Connecticut. Or if you've a mind to, spend the next two evenings with me. The countryside is now aglow with exceptionally ecstatic fall splendor. Why not join me and see if we can effect a suitable metaphor for such an autumnally florid frenzy?"

I was about to hang up when a horrid impulse overcame me and the following phrase just erupted from my center and went hurtling indelibly upon the magnetic spool of Marion's device: "Will you marry me?"

Then I hung up.

Hmmmmm, it's too late now, I thought. Like a letter in the mailbox, I've passed the point of no return.

I thought a brisk walk in the Connecticut evening might bring me to my senses, might provide me with a suitable avenue of retreat.

Yes, I thought, I need a great deal of fresh air. This stuffy room has gone to my brain.

I dressed quickly and walked from the cottage house suite into the dark night of Salisbury.

XXVIII

WHAT IF SHE ACCEPTS? I asked myself as I passed through the light rays that filtered from the inn's restaurant. What if she actually wants to engage in such a disastrous enterprise?

The most horrifying detail of this fiasco was that I had made my request in a state of relative sobriety.

There in the brisk night air of an autumnal Connecticut village, I observed how easily prone I was to hysteria. From a simply foolish slip of my common sense I was plunged into such a paranoid vision of pain and imprisonment that I had to stop in my tracks to collect myself.

This is ridiculous, I thought. Marion can't possibly take me seriously. And even if she does, I will simply tell her I didn't mean what I said. She'll ask the obvious question, such as "Why did you say it then?," and I will slide my way out of the entire mess by telling her how overwhelmed I've been by my feelings of love for her.

"That's the reason most men give for wanting to marry."

This was said not, as I would like to have imagined, as my own inner dialogue, but actually by Marion. She had arrived at the White Hart the very next afternoon. Our conversation, after my disgracefully insincere exclamations of joy at seeing her, soon dwindled into an argument when she saw the truth beneath the frozen smile.

"What are you afraid of, J.C.?" she asked with barely contained fury.

"You're too young for me."

And she was. That's true. She was thirty-one and I pressing the near side of my fifty-third birthday.

"I am old enough to be your father."

"That's what I love about you."

"Oh, really!" I flamed. "And when that amusement wears off?!"

"You will just have to endure my middle-age crises as best you can."

"In your forties, Marion, I'll be pushing seventy."

"You look ten years younger than you are," she offered as some consolation.

"Oh," I flamed again, "so you *have* thought of my age!"

"Of course I have. It was the first thing to look at when you asked me," she said quickly. "Oh, and I saved it, J.C. The message recording of your proposal. I may even have copies of it sent around if you back out."

I almost thought her serious until she began to smile joyously at my discomfort.

"Oh, thank God you're joking, Marion."

"No, I'm not," she said. "Just because I enjoy your embarrassment doesn't mean I'm not holding you to your word. It will be my agreeable pastime to see you try and squirm your way out of this."

"Marion," I implored, "have you really considered the implications, the repercussions, the utterly untenable nature of a marriage between the two of us?"

"Then I ask again! Why did you propose?"

"I love you, Marion. It was the foolish culmination of some very sincere feelings of affection for you."

"Affection?! Now it's just affection?!"

"No, I love you. I've said it now at least five times. And it's *because* I love you that I know we can't get married. It would be the ruin of both of us. If you think I drink *now*, just imagine what a disastrous marriage might do to me!"

"What makes you think it would be a disaster, J.C.?"

After a moment of hunting for the most convincing explanation, I replied: "Our love. We love each other too much to get married. Lovers are doomed to be failures as husband and wife. It's a fact."

"What fact? Name some examples."

"Romeo and Juliet!"

"They're fiction."

I began to hunt for examples but they all appeared to be either from novels or movies like *The Blue Angel*.

"Oh," I sighed with relief, "Zelda and F. Scott Fitzgerald! An utter disaster! An Armageddon of a marriage!"

"They were both borderline, J.C.! Beyond the help of even the best therapists!"

"Oh," I double flamed, "you are going to therapize us into a successful marriage?!"

"It wouldn't hurt," she said. "A bit of our own medicine might help us."

175

"I can give that to you for free, Marion! If you want to set up regular sessions with me—"

"Don't be ridiculous, J.C. You're the last psychiatrist I'd see."

"Really?!!!"

"Yes. You are the exact opposite of what I would need in a therapist."

"Oh, I am, am I? But I am precisely what you need in a husband?!"

"No," she said immediately. "You're just as unpromising in that respect."

"Then why would you ever want to marry me?"

Tears rose to her eyes and the following poured out of her in a wave: "I love you, J.C. I didn't want to, don't want to, would do anything not to be in love with you, but I just can't help it. It's excruciating to think that I can't get you out of my mind, and when I heard your voice on the tape say, 'Will you marry me?,' I began to weep with such joy and anger. I couldn't understand my reaction. I would have hoped to be calm and realistic. Flattered, but certain of the impossibility. Instead I felt that there'd never be another feeling this great in me for any other man, that you are the only human being to have stopped me right in my tracks and made me forget myself and my intelligence and my achievements and my power. I'm a powerful creature, J.C.!"

"I know that, Marion," I said through my own veil of tears.

"I'm afraid of my arrogance and my certainty. You make me very uncertain and very confused and very ex-

176

cited and very worried and very humble and I don't want to lose that, J.C. I'd risk even a disastrous marriage for that. And now you tell me that you're not serious and I don't believe it. Not for a minute. You feel the same as I do and—"

At this point, my lips became glued forcefully to those of Marion and what followed was disastrous for the clothes we were wearing but very rejuvenating to our sense of health and well-being.

In the aftermath, thoughts of Anaïs Nin once again crept in.

"Marion," I asked, "did Charlotte Manes ever try to seduce you?"

I had expected a shocked and possibly angry reaction. However, following a brief pause, Marion's voice struck my ears with blinding simplicity.

"Yes."

At this, of course, I rose to a seated position on the bed and looked at her.

I waited. For some explanation.

I waited.

And waited.

"Marion," I said rather too firmly, "what do you mean by that?"

She smiled.

"You expect me to describe seduction to you, J.C.? You would like me to recall for Rembrandt the art of the self-portrait?"

"Marion, don't make light of this. It's a terribly serious thing we're discussing."

"It certainly is," she said while joining me in a bed-top pow-wow. "And she was very good at it."

I looked at her even more closely.

"Good at what?"

"Seduction."

After a squeamish pause, I asked: "How good?"

"I had fantasies of kissing her. Dreams, actually."

I nodded, waiting for the dreaded confession.

"And . . . ?"

"And what?" I gave her my severest, no-nonsense, I-might-leave-you-this-minute-if-you-don't-answer-me expression.

"You really are scared, J.C." It was a declaration, not a question.

"Marion," I said, now pointing my finger almost in her face, "anything like this could make you a suspect in the murder of Charlotte Manes, you know that?"

She rose and began to put her clothes on rather briskly.

"In all my life," she began, "I have never been quite this insulted."

Her blouse went on first.

"Charlotte Manes was one of the saddest, sickest cases I have ever encountered! Despite anything my subconscious might dredge up in a dream . . ."

Her jeans were now being filled slowly, jerkily, and at times, it would seem, painfully.

". . . and despite your own salacious inventories—"

"Marion," I began to implore, "I have been reading Anaïs Nin's 1933 diary."

"Oh, you have, have you?!!!"

178

This came as her sweater was being forcibly pulled over her head. She shook her perfectly tailored boy's cut out. The raven black hairs fell pertly into place.

"There seemed to be no one, Marion, that she couldn't take to bed if she put her mind to it. Including her own father!

"Oh, and her father had nothing to do with that?!"

"She was thirty years old by then!"

"And her father a blithering idiot? A man who had no control over his 'raging, sexual member'?!"

She uttered this last quote like a sarcastic three-year-old.

"Marion, she compromised *both* of her analysts!"

Here is where Marion stopped her progress.

"Oh! So, any incest victim becomes some kind of primal monster?! Exuding such sexuality that God Himself could not resist?!"

I was suitably humbled by this outburst to not speak, so she continued.

"You are right, J.C. Any marriage between us would be a disaster. How could you question my integrity?! And from reading the lurid confessions of a borderline personality like Miss Nin's?"

"What do you mean?" I asked. "Are you saying Miss Nin was a functioning psychotic?"

"The way I feel now," warned Marion with blazing eyes, "*I'm* a functioning psychotic and just possibly willing to pay the price for kicking you right in the teeth."

By now she had her boots on and the potential for some serious damage had increased commensurately.

"No, I did not have an affair with *any* of my clients. Beyond a simple handshake, I have not even touched them. But since you have forced me to make such an embarrassing and utterly unnecessary assertion, I vow never to see or speak to you again."

With that she was out the door.

XXIX

THE COCKTAIL LOUNGE OF THE Westbury Hotel is a perfect stopping place after the quintessential fall purchase at Ralph Lauren: a tweed sport jacket. I only buy extra-long. Once I had put one on by accident. It was then I realized that destiny had no other port in store for me but a forty-two or forty-three extra-long. The size variables are contingent upon my gustatory self-discipline. This year of Our Lord, 1993, has proven to be a tribute to the heftier size, the broader and more portly soulful dimension.

No, I haven't grown fat exactly. I have just tended to carry my seniority with a denser solemnity.

What was I doing in the cocktail lounge of the Westbury Hotel?

I had phoned Dr. Lodge and decided to have a showdown of sorts. I expected him to decline, to wheedle his way out of the gauntlet I'd thrown down.

"I'm certain of a few things now," I had said into the pay phone, "and I would prefer to disclose them face-to-face."

He immediately responded: "Strange you should call, Dr. Kaminer. I have a few of my own conclusions to share. Where shall we meet?"

I suggested the Westbury and he agreed.

I arrived early so that I could enjoy my daily Lillet in peace. I knew I'd be ordering coffee the minute Dr. Lodge arrived. I would try to convince him of the sobriety of my concerns. I hoped he would decline and order himself something as conducive to disclosing secrets as a very dry double martini.

He did precisely that.

"Two olives, please," he added as the waiter began to leave.

I envied the glow that rose in his face as the gin slipped smoothly down his throat.

"You're a martini drinker," I offered as an opening to our conversation.

"Yes," he said happily. "Have been all of my adult life. It gets away from me occasionally but. . . ."

"How do you mean 'gets away from you?'"

"Once every three months or so, I find myself breaking my limit of one martini."

"One *double* martini, sir?"

"Yes," he replied, smiling a bit testily. "One double."

"What was the date of your last excess?"

"Oh," he grinned rather cavalierly, "about three months ago."

"Then I might have something to look forward to."

"Not if you don't drink yourself," he said, looking disparagingly at my small pot of coffee. "I never embarrass myself without company."

"Let's exchange seriousnesses, sir, and then see what extravagances are inspired in either of us."

"Fine," he said.

"I am increasingly convinced," I began, "that you, Doctor, are the only possible person, aside from my client, with motive and anger enough to silence Charlotte Manes."

He looked at me over the martini glass and then asked: "With a kitchen knife?"

Hmmmm, I thought, that is odd. Something I hadn't really included in the mix, as they say.

"I might use a scalpel, an overdose of some prescription drug, an undetectable invader of the heart or the brain—there's an almost endless set of possibilities for a murder weapon. But a kitchen knife?"

I noticed that Dr. Lodge's eloquence had increased since our last meeting. He seemed to have found my own purple proclivities infectious.

"An argument occurred," I offered, "in your very own kitchen, perhaps."

"In Manhattan," he reminded me. "Her body was found in Connecticut."

"You drove her there to divert suspicion."

"To whom?" he asked calmly.

Hmmmm, another seeming cul de sac.

We both waited in silence.

It was at that point that I ordered my *own* double mar-

183

tini. False accusations are not my favorite cocktail conversation and having, perhaps, begun this with a whopper, accusing Dr. Lodge of murder, I decided to abandon sober judgment and explore the more luxurious option of a drunken intuition. I hadn't braved a martini in at least five years. It was one of my more righteous secrets, comforting in the sense of its almost cost-free sacrifice. The prospect of a *double* martini, however, ensured that I would pay some price the following morning.

"Cheers," I said as I raised the libation to my lips.

There followed a pleasurable burning sensation, followed by a spreading warmth throughout my chest.

"Hmmmm," I murmured, "I'd forgotten how uniquely persuasive the imagination can be. I could have sworn there was vermouth in here."

"The olives help," smiled Dr. Lodge. "They're about as close to Italy as this gin will ever get."

I realized then that we shared a similar addiction, not just to alcohol, but also to the incredibly fine distinctions some people make in order to prolong the rite of tasteful inebriation. Or as my uncle Henry used to call it, getting "aesthetically sloshed." He was the ultimate master of such graceful dissipation. There was a kind of poetry to the reek of wine in his pores.

After savoring the full effect of the double martini, after allowing its first winsome invasion to color our spirits, Dr. Lodge and I embarked on the heart of our conversation.

"The abortion," I said.

Dr. Lodge's eyes lifted from his glass.

"Charlotte's abortion. What do you know of it?"

"She had it. And in the aftermath, and for some reason I still can't comprehend, she came to me for help."

"She never told you her thoughts about it?" I asked. "Never explained why she chose you?"

"I can tell you *her* explanation. 'You're the only person,' she said, 'that could get my father to do the right thing.'"

I waited for him to continue, but he returned, rather too quickly, to his drink.

"And you accepted that?" I asked in mild shock.

"No, of course not. But it never occurred to me that she was bent on destroying me because, in her subconscious mind, I had taken her father away from her."

Again I waited, but by now Dr. Gordon had finished his first double martini and was raising his arm for the second one.

I continued to wait.

"I told her that," he finally said.

"What?"

"That our relationship could only destroy me and that perhaps that's what she was after all the time. Revenge."

Again he sipped quickly from the fresh martini.

"It was then she told me that sex could never be as good as it had been with her father."

He looked up at me—for what I'm not sure. An agreement of some sort. His eyes seemed to be asking simultaneously for forgiveness and ridicule.

185

"Then she belittled me in a long tirade about how disappointing a lover I had proven. It appears I showed none of the expertise her father had."

Again another sip.

"I never saw her again after that."

It was at that point that I returned to my own martini, looking for somewhat the same courage Dr. Lodge seemed to be finding in his.

"How did you know," I then asked, "that Charlotte had been seeing Marion Brockman?"

"Marion told me. At her interview."

He stopped there. Thought a bit, and instead of continuing, returned to his martini.

I found myself cursing the depth of my gallantry.

"What did she tell you?"

"When I began to explain to her the enormous requirements of her possible caseload, that they might well include cancer and AIDS patients and a whole list of physical disabilities with which I found her experience sorely lacking, I think she smelled my rejection."

"I had rejected *him*, J.C.!" had proclaimed the naked and most unmatronly maid Marion in the center of our hotel room at the White Hart on the preceding weekend. "The outrage, that he cloaks his philandering vengeance under professional standards. Despicable!!!"

These sounds were ringing in my ears as Dr. Lodge continued his tale at the Westbury over the dwindling remains of his second double martini.

"I think she knew I was not going to approve her application."

"Hmmm," I murmured through the effects of my own martini, "she claims you attempted to date her first."

After looking quickly at me, he said: "I don't deny the request, but I do deny its connection to this interview."

He paused.

I waited.

"That would explain, however, why she told me that she had been seeing Charlotte Benedict."

"I'm not sure I follow you, Doctor."

"Ov-biously," he said with a slur, and then corrected himself. "Obviously, she must have learned of my affair with Charlotte and was using that to blackmail me."

"Blackmail you?" I said with a certain mounting anger. "Into what?"

"Into approving her application."

I cleaned my teeth with my tongue. It is a particularly telling psychological gesture in me. It most likely means that I would prefer to see a bullet entering your brain, a sharp object dividing your head from your neck, or any possible series of extremely drastic kinds of murder and/or mutilation happening to you than to hear whatever it was you just said to provoke the aforementioned gesture, or as some like to call it, nervous habit.

After a few deep breaths to contain my rage and my own growing inebriation, I said: "Dr. Lodge? I know something of the lady, the, uh, exceptional and finely tuned human being we are referring to, and if you will allow me a possible explanation, I believe Ms. Brockman chose to remind you, in the most eloquent way possible, of your *own* lapses in professional quality. Your *own* egre-

187

gious derelictions of duty. Your *own* shocking and, I might add, almost unforgivable abuse of power—not only with your patient Charlotte Benedict, but with Dr. Brockman as well."

I continued, rolling over his lame efforts at objecting: "Because despite your present and very convincing display of regret, I do believe you have a moral flaw centered so deeply within you that God Himself might find it intimidating to remedy."

It was at this point that Dr. Lodge's tears began to flow. They ran so copiously and fluidly that I feared he might refill his double martini glass with them. A few bystanders began to notice the display as they exited the room.

"We're havin' a lovers' spat," I offered by way of explanation.

At first Dr. Lodge's eyes widened with horror at my words and then he seemed to comprehend his utterly untenable moral posturing and he began to laugh. The laughter grew in very graceful proportions to a very infectious symphony of sound that had the headwaiter both amused and disturbed.

"Forgive me," Dr. Lodge continued through the tears that now seemed to spring from hilarity, "I will find a way to control myself. It's just that I'm having one of the best times of my life and I will be eternally grateful to my friend here"—at this point he paused and with a witty rhythm, winked at me gaily—"for putting my entire life in perspective."

"Fine," said the headwaiter embarrassedly and left.

"I don't think I need order another martini," Dr. Lodge said meekly.

"Perhaps dinner then," I offered.

He looked at me with some surprise. "You'll dine again with such a moral idiot, a reprobate like myself?"

"I'm a physician, Doctor. It's part of my oath to tend the sick and unfortunate."

XXX

By the time dr. lodge had reached his crème brûlée and his double espresso—he is a man who sobers up as seriously as he drinks—he was fairly brimming over with joy and bonhomie. It corroborated my suspicion about the resilience of health, that it has nothing to do with the melancholy side effects attending the more scrupulous and morally sensitive members of our race. I had visions of Dr. Mengele happily wolfing down buckets of paella in the more habitable jungles of Ecuador.

By this time in the evening I had learned the following: aside from being an incorrigible lady's man, Dr. Lodge had more gossip in him than my great-aunt Medora. She could relay the incipient scandals of Bremington, South Carolina, with the speed of an auctioneer. I never understood why American actors make Southern people talk so slowly. A New Jersey car salesman would be hard put to compete with *any* talk in my family, let alone that of Great-aunt Medora. I've heard her rattle off the entire "Insiders" column of the *Bremington Record*'s Style Section in one breath. Dr. Lodge's revelations came in more sporadic offerings, teasing parcels of rumor and, in some cases, flagrant calumny. Or so I thought.

"Charley's mother demanded the abortion," he said.

"You know that firsthand?" I challenged.

"She told me that the day our affair began. I don't know why I found it so persuasive, but with the image of her father abusing her and her mother dictating the most important decisions of her life, I guess I found her an irresistible victim."

"Why would her mother have that kind of power?"

"Charley's inheritance. Most of the money's on her mother's side."

By now I had finished my profiterole. If I'm terribly abstemious in my entree—i.e., grilled sole or chicken, with rice or a boiled potato, the kind of meal you see on the cover of those horrible frozen diet dinners—I occasionally reward myself with an incredibly disastrous dessert. I was just licking the remnants of a particularly impressive chocolate sauce from my spoon when it occurred to me that Dr. Lodge's gossip didn't fit the Charlotte Benedict I had encountered in my office. Dr. Lodge agreed.

"Oh, you're right, Doctor. By the time you met her, I believe Charlotte was beyond blackmail of any kind."

"Blackmail? You mean her mother actually threatened to disinherit her?"

"Yes," said the doctor between sips of his coffee. "Mrs. Benedict has an actual phobia about African Americans."

"So she told me," I mused. "Not the least bit ashamed about it, either."

"You spoke with her about it?"

"Yes, I went there to talk about Charlotte and Charles, and I walked into a veritable hornet's nest of hatred. Unfortunately, I was the one to reveal that Charley was an incest victim."

"I beg your pardon," said the doctor.

"She learned about the molestation from me."

Dr. Lodge's response to this conveyed such simultaneous volumes of surprise and scorn that I count it one of the most embarrassing moments in my professional life. After what seemed decades of silence, the doctor smugly offered his condolences.

"You are an amazing creature, Dr. Kaminer. You've proven yourself one of the most adroit and worldly minds I've ever encountered. Also one of the most considerate, and it is, perhaps, that gift which has led you astray. Mrs. Benedict, I'm afraid to say, has known of her daughter's plight for some time now. At least since the middle of my *own* affair with Charley."

I couldn't believe it, and yet I had to. There was no motive for Dr. Lodge to lie in this respect and all the reason in the world for Charlotte's mother to pretend innocence. It was, however, the depth of shock she conveyed that had convinced me.

"You've gone quite pale, J.C.," said Dr. Lodge.

I would have taken exception to his calling me by my initials, but I was, indeed, too stunned by the news.

"What makes you so certain of that?" I finally asked him.

"The phrase," began Dr. Lodge, "was, I think, 'I would

have aborted *you*, Charley, had I known this would happen.' Mrs. Benedict said that right after Charley told her."

"Told her what?"

"That her father had molested her."

My ailing appearance obviously hadn't changed since Dr. Lodge remarked on it. "I'm sorry this disturbs you so, Doctor."

"I actually like Mrs. Benedict. Despite her pride and prejudice, or perhaps because of it, I could sympathize. I just find it hard to believe that she was lying about her ignorance. Oh, I know subliminally we all grasp much more than we'd like to, but in this case, I truly believed that she hadn't the slightest conscious notion about her husband's and her daughter's incest."

Dr. Lodge seemed to be waiting respectfully for me to put together the inferences he had so clearly inspired.

"Incest," he murmured. "And infanticide?"

"Charlotte was hardly an infant, Doctor."

"Please call me Martin."

Something in his ensuing silence acknowledged my profound inability to do that.

"You actually despise me, don't you, Doctor."

"If I could, I would will you to be the killer. It would make life so much simpler. People I congenitally loathe all lumped together in the county jail awaiting arraignment. Unfortunately, God has made it impossible to clean our lives out in the same way we vacuum our homes."

"Well, on that cheery note, I suggest we split the bill. I

193

had considered you my guest until those last few unfortunate words."

"The bill's been paid," I said. "I refuse to put myself in your debt for our lunch at the Manhattan Athletic Club."

"Am I now in *your* debt?" he replied.

"No. My insults, I suppose, make us just about even."

XXXI

I HAD SO WANTED DR. LODGE to be the guilty party.

"Marion?" I said meekly into the phone.

Click came the response.

I dialed again.

After numerous rings the phone picked up.

"I love you!" I exclaimed immediately and waited for the click. It didn't come. To ensure any further longevity to this call, I continued: "I love you, I love you, I love you!! And I am in agony over my own suspicion—"

"J.C.," she interrupted quietly. "I think you need help."

"I need *you*, Marion!"

There was a silence at the end of the line.

"I need you. And I *do* want to marry you. I confess that unreservedly."

"You love me so much," came the deadeningly quiet voice, "that you'd risk marrying a killer?"

"Marion, you are not the killer and I—"

"You don't think so, J.C.? Why? I'm not capable of plunging a knife into someone? I felt like it last weekend."

"I know, Marion. . . ."

195

"I could have done worse than that, you know?"

"I know, Marion."

"You've had those feelings, J.C.?"

"Yes, Marion."

"Anger so great you'd like the person you thought you loved—you'd like them drawn and quartered before your very own eyes?"

"Of course, Marion. I've had similar feelings."

"About me?" she asked quickly.

"No, Marion. About some of the people I've encountered in this little investigation."

"So you don't love me enough to want me dead?"

After a slight pause, I said: "At this point, Marion, no. That could be a shortcoming on my side, but who knows what the future might bring?"

"Yes, J.C.," she said. "Seeing you again might fuel whole reservoirs of possible revenge. I might succeed in making you twice as homicidal as you made me."

"I know, Marion."

"Why are you so certain I, Mrs. Charlotte Manes' analyst, didn't break every code of ethics known to medicine and fall into bed with my client and then, in my guilty fear and jealousy over her many other infidelities, murder her? Slice her open with a kitchen knife?"

"Because I think I know who did it, but I have some questions only you can answer. Can we meet?"

After a pause, she said: "At my office. In twenty minutes."

XXXII

"WHERE ARE THE POLICE IN all this?" asked Marion as she sat stiffly at her desk.

"Charles might know," I replied from the visitor's chair. "I meet with him tomorrow morning. I hope. He has canceled the last three appointments and left some very strange messages on my answering machine. The only comforting news about him is his scoring. He's led the league in most points scored per game for the last five matches."

"What was that quote from Martin Lodge?" interrupted Marion.

"Charley's words?"

"Yes."

"She told him her mother said: 'I would have had *you* aborted if I'd known this would happen.' Something like that."

Marion rose from her desk and went to her files. Within minutes she returned with some spiral notebooks, all dated and neatly ordered chronologically.

"I think," she said as she flipped through their pages,

"that Charlotte said something like that to me, but it had nothing to do with her father."

She paused from her activity and looked up at me.

"I've had two sessions with Mrs. Benedict since we've spoken and I firmly believe that she knew nothing consciously of her daughter's incest."

I felt relieved.

Marion sat and read quietly through two of her little journals.

"Yes, here it is," she said. "On March eighth, she said: 'My mother threatened to disinherit me.'"

Marion read this to me and then looked up.

"I remember now," she continued. "I had asked her about children. Why hadn't she and Charles had any children? And that is when this quote arose. But it had nothing to do with the affair. She never told me she'd even mentioned incest to her mother."

"How," I questioned, "did this quote arise, Marion?"

She consulted her notes.

"I had asked her what her mother had actually said. 'Have the child aborted,' she said. 'I will not be the grandmother to a pickaninny.'"

I couldn't believe I was hearing the word 'pickaninny' outside of a movie theater, north of the Mason-Dixon Line or anywhere post-1963.

"'If I'd known this would happen,'" read Marion from one of her diaries, "'I'd have had you aborted.'"

I began to nod to myself in a way that told me the key was here, lodged permanently in this information. I don't think my way to a conclusion. I watch my body respond to information and when it's moved to make such clear and unequivocal gestures I know the vote is in, so to speak; that every little backwater fiber of my being has cast its ballots.

"Marion," I asked, "how many times did Charlotte have an abortion?"

"Many, I suspect, but how often is hard to tell. She only spoke of this one time."

"What date was that?"

"Shortly after they married—nineteen seventy-nine or eighty, I believe."

"Is it possible she became pregnant recently? I mean as recently as the time of her death?"

Marion's head was arrested in immediate concentration, and then began to twist slowly to indicate no.

"No," she said. "I would have known that. I expect she would have told me."

"You're certain of that?"

Again her head was motionless. Finally, she said: "No. I can't be that certain."

"Why?"

"I recall a very small but disturbing smile on Charlotte's face the last few weeks of our sessions together."

She returned to her diary.

"I even noted it," she said, looking through one of them. "Yes."

She began to read from her notes.

"July: Charlotte projects a secret. Her composure disturbing. Inappropriate affect for where we are in therapy. July: Still the surprising sense of confidence. She says it's the sessions. I know it's too soon. August: Tears. From the beginning of the session to the end. Not a breakthrough. Answers evasive and resentful."

Marion looked up.

"That was our last session."

"I have to talk to Charles," I said. "Charles might know. Or his lawyer."

XXXIII

"Mr. Meyer?"

"Yes, Doctor?"

"Do you have the findings of the autopsy?"

"Yes."

"I'm not sure of the protocol here, but I would like to know one thing: was Charlotte Manes pregnant when she died?"

There was a disturbing pause on the end of the line.

And then an even more disturbing reply.

"Why do you ask?" came Mr. Meyer's suddenly formal tones.

"You know damn well why I ask, Mr. Meyer."

"Yes. Yes, Charlotte Manes was pregnant."

Another pause.

"Does Charles know?"

"Of course. The police tried to use it against him in their investigation. Implied the child might not have been his and that was a motive. I'm surprised he didn't tell you."

"So am I, Mr. Meyer. So am I."

XXXIV

"CHARLES?"

"Hmmm," he said lazily from the couch. He was sprawled there as if on Verradero Beach.

"Mr. Meyer tells me that Charlotte was pregnant when she died."

His head turned toward me, and after a brief glance, his eyes began to wander as if looking for a way out. After a bit of these mildly panicked twitchings, he sat up.

"Yes, Doctor. She was pregnant."

"Why didn't you tell me?"

"You never asked."

I could have hit him. There are times the countertransference becomes so great you doubt your own sanity. Despite his huge size and hulking demeanor, I could have slapped him as if he were a sassing, snot-nosed fifteen-year-old.

I rose from my desk and walked the room a bit to cool off. After sitting down, I said: "Charles, it is obvious you have used these sessions for the last three and three quarter years to hide in. I don't see from your present attitude even one stitch of progress."

"Fine," he said simply. Then he got up and began to leave. At the door he turned.

"I didn't do it. Despite what you think, I didn't kill her. Sure, I didn't know if the child was mine or not, but would that have been so new?"

"Yes, if she were determined to carry the child to term. To give birth to it. Where would that leave you? The laughingstock of the NBA. She could have spawned a child whiter than your Nikes."

"She said it was mine. Came home all happy and crying with joy."

At this point, tears began to appear in his eyes, and he moved slowly back to the couch.

"She told me she'd done it on purpose. Knew exactly when the child had been conceived. Said she loved me. She wanted me to be happy and smiling, but of course, I couldn't trust her. She'd never told me the truth before." He paused. "Why should I believe her then?"

"Did you *ever* want a child?"

"Sure. Second we got married she got pregnant. I was the happiest man alive, and then she had a miscarriage."

There are times in a physician's life when he or she would rather be sitting in the arms of Lucifer himself than have to decide whether or not to tell someone the truth. Should I be the one to give him the news that his mother-in-law had, in effect, ordered the abortion of his own child? But then, at what point do we stop patroniz-

203

ing those we are attempting to strengthen? I was about to reveal that truth, when Charles continued: "But I knew that wasn't true, either. Despite all of her games, Charlotte really hadn't learned how to lie well."

"You mean she'd had an abortion?"

He nodded. "Sure. There was no doctor around to tell me the truth. He just seemed to up and disappear."

"The obstetrician?"

"Uh-huh," he murmured.

"Do you know why she might have had the abortion?" I asked.

"Sure, she didn't know whose baby it was. Like you said, it could prove real embarrassing for all of us."

"Charles," I began, "that was simply my way of pointing out your possible motives for killing her."

"You know 'em all now," he said.

"Well, I don't think this last one is true. I have it on fairly good authority that the reason behind the abortion had more to do with your mother-in-law than with Charlotte's promiscuity."

Charles looked at me with the cautioned dread of someone hearing the sound of his own worst suspicions.

I continued: "Yes, as I understand it, Mrs. Benedict threatened to disinherit Charlotte if she gave birth to your child."

After thinking this through a bit, Charles said: "So what if she did stop all of her money? I had plenty. Before it's all over I'll probably be worth a lot more than her."

"That may be true, but it obviously wasn't as big a certainty to Charlotte."

Charles shook his head in disgust. "'Five days,' her mother used to say. 'This marriage'll last five days.'"

"You think Charlotte believed her?"

"I don't know what the bitch believed and I don't care." This was the first time Charles had ever used that particular term of unendearment about his wife.

"Cunt," he said contemptuously. "Cunt, bitch, cocksucking slut, whore. She'd have blown the barnyard if I'd owned a farm. Fucked the whole stable if I'd raced horses."

At this point he began to look for something he could do some damage to. I did not want to be included in the inventory.

"Charles," I began, hoping to slow him down.

"You slip all this shit to me about her maybe carrying my child?"

"It's a possibility, Charles, and—"

"So is the end of the world, Doc, but I'm still calling it a long shot in *my* lifetime. That bitch couldn't know whose child was in her, ever."

"You're sure of that?"

"Yeah. Yeah, sure. Sure I'm sure." He spoke with quickly dwindling certainty.

"You don't think the times that she said she was pregnant with your child . . . ?"

Here he stood to his full and towering height and took a few frighteningly full breaths.

"You don't think," I continued cautiously, "that she might actually have been telling the truth?"

Somewhere within my very formidable patient there

205

was a destruction going on, a very embarrassing surrender. Within him defenses were being dismantled with alarming speed. He began a sound which seemed a moan until he endeavored to turn it into clearing his throat. This little ruse faded into a few additional and lame-sounding politenesses. Then another, slightly longer moan came. "Hmmmmm-hmmmmmmm." The sound emerged from between his pursed lips.

He sat down again. "Doctor," he said a little too loudly and with another of those throat clearings, "I don't think you should be doing this to me right now."

"Doing what, Charles?"

"Trying to reinstate a faith in my wife that I doubt I ever had."

"Then why did you marry her?"

After a pause, he said: "I loved her."

Another pause.

"I loved her so much that even my fears couldn't keep me from marrying her. And obviously, I still must be loving her because all this bullshit about her telling the truth is cutting a hole right through my chest and sticking a knife in a place I'd forgotten about for some time now."

"Did you love her enough to kill her, Charles?"

"Yes."

He looked at me directly and with a sense of expectation. As if I'd shortly have the phone in my hands, dialing 911. Then he added.

"But I didn't. You keep asking me the same thing and I'm telling you for the last time I didn't do it. I didn't kill my wife."

206

XXXV

"DOCTOR?" CAME THE VOICE THROUGH the phone.

"Yes?"

"This is Dooby."

Hmmmm, I wondered. What is this about?

"Can we meet?"

"Yes. I'm free tomorrow afternoon."

"No, right now. It's real important."

"Where are you now?"

"The New York Health and Racquet Club on West Fifty-Sixth Street."

"There's a French restaurant on Sixty-third and Madison. Le Relais. I'll be there in twenty minutes."

When I arrived, Dooby was standing near the little bar at the front sipping a Perrier. He looked worried.

"Dooby?"

"Hi, Doc. Can we sit? Privately."

"Hello, Doctor," said the maître d'. "You know the lunch hour is over."

"I understand, but is there a table in the back we can use? It's a rather important matter we have to discuss and I'd like some privacy."

207

"Certainly," he said as he led us to the back of the small and empty restaurant.

"Thanks, Doc. I know it's short notice but you'll understand, I think."

"I'm sure I will, Dooby."

"You saw Charles just yesterday, right?"

"Yes."

"Well, he's just lost it. I mean, I guess you got him thinkin' in some pretty dangerous directions."

I waited for him to clarify himself. It was taking him some time to collect his thoughts.

"Well, to get right to the point, he wants me to kill Mrs. Benedict. Charlotte's mother. He wants me to put her away."

Hmmm, I thought. Dooby says this as if it were a service he could offer anyone.

"Dooby? I didn't know you offered those services."

"I don't. But you don't stay in the bodyguard business without giving the impression that you might, you know? Who's gonna take you seriously if you aren't willing to go all the way?"

This explanation, despite its novelty and bloodcurdling simplicity, seemed almost indisputable.

"How did he propose this, Dooby?"

"What do you mean?"

"What reason, if any, did he offer for his desire to have Mrs. Benedict disposed of?"

Dooby looked at me like he might a snake in the weeds, for that is unquestionably what I had become.

"Come on, Doc, don't get dumb on me. You've got

Charles believing his wife loved him and wanted to have his kid and God knows what else."

He ended with a scoffing wag of the head that indicated the world had gone, if not crazy, at least unforgivably sentimental.

"Even *I* got into her pants," he added out of the side of his mouth.

"You mean this could have been *your* child?"

"Naw," he whined. "We just got it off in the back of the car one night. She was drunk and I was horny and that was it. Kid stuff. No big deal, but nothin' I'd tell Charles about."

"But you'd like to."

"What?"

"You'd like to let him know what a whore she was."

"Right! Goddamn right, when he wants to go shooting her mother for givin' her some damn good advice. That bitch could no more raise her own baby than keep her eyes off of every man she ever met."

There was something in Dooby's furtive certainty that sickened me. He had an anger over Charlotte Benedict almost the equal of his employer's now diverted rage.

"What have you told Charles?"

"About what?"

"Well, did you agree to shoot the poor woman?"

He looked at me as if to take exception at my pity for Charlotte's mother.

"I said I'd think about it."

"Did he offer you money?"

"No."

"Isn't that a normal part of these bargains?"

"Not between friends."

Is this, I wondered, a can of worms, a Pandorian box worth opening?

"He'd pay me something. Sure. But that's not what I was thinking of, you know?"

I nodded in a kind of partial understanding.

"I'm wondering," he continued, "where the hell this is gonna get us? He's got one murder charge on him, and now he wants to go adding another. You gotta talk to him. You gotta cool him off."

I sat in silence for a moment.

"Dooby? Do you think Charles killed his wife?"

"I didn't used to. But now, who the hell knows? He's been acting so wacky lately. You gave him a whole thing about Christ that had him off the wall for about a week. I had a hard time getting him back on Earth. Haven't you noticed?"

"Well," I offered, "after that session, he left some very strange messages on my phone machine, and he did begin our last meeting with a really bizarre attitude, considering his predicament."

"Right! That's it. He's lost it, like I said. Get him into a hospital. Drug him. Bring him down. 'Cause if *I* don't take care of Mrs. Benedict, he might."

"You really think so?"

"He said, 'Dooby, I'm not a victim anymore.'"

Dooby by now was looking me directly in the eye.

"Scared me, Doc. The way he said it? Cold. He looked like a block of ice."

"Where is he now, Dooby?"

"Home," he said. And then added, "I hope."

Dooby waited patiently while I reviewed my options.

"We have an appointment on Friday, Dooby."

"That's almost two days off, Doc. Pretty risky."

"Tell him you won't do it. Tell him what you told me, that you think he's crazy and ought to be locked up."

"Oh, great, great. I tell him that and he goes off and shoots his mother-in-law."

"Does he have a gun of his own?"

"No, but he'll ask for mine."

"Don't give it to him."

"Besides," he added, "he wouldn't need one. Wouldn't take much to put that old bag away."

"I'm not about to call him, Dooby. We've spent too many years trying to put him on his own feet, into his own best judgment. I'm not going to intrude on that."

"Shooting some ole lady's gonna make a man out of him?!"

"That's not what I mean, Dooby, and you know it."

"But what if he did do that? What if he just put the lady away?"

"Therapy, Dooby, like anything else in life, is a risk."

"I'm thinking," he said with a suspicious look at me, "that I should be going to the police."

"Maybe you should, and maybe you shouldn't. That's your business."

XXXVI

"Mrs. benedict?"

"Yes," came her very deep and slightly drunken voice.

"May I see you?"

A pause.

"Who *are* you?" she asked, a smile in her tone and a flirtatious innuendo in the contralto lilt.

"Kaminer, J. C. Kaminer."

Another pause.

"Fine," came the voice.

"This afternoon?"

"I'll be in all day."

This came in a playful singsong.

XXXVII

HER LAWN STILL HADN'T BEEN tended and the facade of her house projected tragedy. How, I'm not sure. Obviously I was painting it with my forebodings.

"Come in," she said with a smile that seemed to come from a belly that now lay partly exposed through her open dressing gown. She was underdressed in a modestly self-conscious bikini, the sort that was fashionable in the sixties.

"Can I get you a drink?" she asked as I followed her into the living room.

I thought, why not? It might keep me from patronizing her.

"Yes, please."

"What'll it be?"

"Scotch. Just a simple bit of scotch on the rocks."

I hadn't tasted scotch in years, but its name rang thrillingly clear through my mind.

She turned with the scotch in her hand, extended it playfully at full length, and then chirped, "So what's up?"

I took the glass from her hand.

213

"You murdered your daughter—didn't you, Mrs. Benedict?"

She paused, and then for some bizarre reason began to look at the backs of her hands, at her fingernails, and then briefly at her palms. She then clasped them together as if satisfied with what she had discovered.

"Yes, I did," she then said simply. "And for all the wrong reasons."

She then turned toward the bar and began to mix her own drink.

"Regardless of that, she's better off dead, and I, in all honesty, haven't felt this good in years. I'm a drunk. And I'm a murderer. And I'm proud of both. There are some things and some people that are just meant to rid the Earth of vermin. That this particular bit of lice happened to be my daughter is incidental."

She then toasted me with her drink.

A martini.

With three olives.

She then sat.

I sat also, directly across from her on the smaller sofa that faced the grand one she was now enthroned in.

Placing one olive pertly in her mouth, she said: "Could you get me a cell next to Leona Helmsley?"

I looked down at my drink, in embarrassment, I suppose. I'm not quite sure how to describe the emotion. Suffice to say, I just had to look away.

"She'll be out in a few weeks I hear and might prove helpful. How *do* the spoiled and pampered adjust to living with the sick and criminal and angry and, oh hell, you get my message."

She then took a very sizeable swallow of her martini.

"Mrs. Benedict," I began, "did it happen here? In Connecticut?"

She looked at me and then grinned a profoundly insincere smile. Her voice dripping acid, she said: "Do you mean did I stab my largest kitchen knife into the heart of my own daughter? In my own home? In my own kitchen?"

I did not answer.

"Of course I did. The knife was conveniently at hand and Charlotte inconveniently unrepentant. I knew she would have that pickaninny brat whether I wanted it or not."

Again another very long drink.

"Mrs. Benedict? Do you want help?"

She looked up at me over her drink. She stared at me for a very long time.

"No," she said simply.

Then she reached in for the second olive and sucked on it, pulling the red pimento out onto her tongue. It sat there the way it would have were Mrs. Benedict seven years old instead of the seventy-something she projected in her very tired and vanquished state.

"You'll be my last audience, Dr. Kaminer. I'm a Catholic. I was, at any rate. A Connecticut Catholic has a certain prestige, particularly if she's wealthy. There's a secret envy for the successfully rigid in this state. And

215

yes, I've been very rigid. I drank—or drink, as you see—
and that is my only really major fault, except, of course,
for succumbing to homicidal rage upon hearing that my
own daughter wanted to make me the grandmother to a
nigger. Where that came from I have no idea. Why God
gave me the scruples of Medea I'll never know. I'll get
my revenge on Him, though. Make no mistake about
that. I'll perform the sin that can't be forgiven and then
my family will see to it that I'm buried in consecrated
ground anyway. That hypocrisy will be added to all the
other my Church has wallowed in, but I will go to my
grave knowing that *I* am not a hypocrite. I loathe the
African American, as he is wont to be called these days.
Don't much care for the Jews either, but I wouldn't murder anyone over it. I am and have been a lot of things,
Dr. Kaminer, but one thing I will not be is a hypocrite. I
never liked sex. Would like to have made love to you,
though, before I go, or so I thought when I met you the
other day. But now that I consider it I find it repulsive.
As repulsive as I always thought sex was. I've had, I
think, all of fifteen orgasms in my life and never
thought them that much to sing about. And the contor-
tions we have to go through to get there don't seem
worth the effort."

It was here she pulled the third and last olive from her
glass. Her look, I imagine, was thrown in to harvest the
effects on me of her shamelessness. I assume my expression conveyed a suitable discomfort and intrigue.

"Mrs. Benedict?" I ventured. "What about Charles?"

"What about him?"

216

"You'd like to go to your grave leaving an innocent man guilty?"

"He's not innocent. He's black. By his very nature he's swollen with sin."

Her head began a little prideful bob and weave. Some part of her nature couldn't take the last statement seriously, so a small but frightened smile began to creep to the corners of her mouth.

Then came the hideous idea that to this day I find hard to believe actually triumphed.

"Mrs. Benedict, if I wrote out a confession, would you sign it?"

She finished the last drops of her drink.

"Depends on what it says."

I then quickly sat down at the living room desk and wrote out on some paper I found there the following words:

> I, Mrs. George Benedict of Ridgefield, Connecticut, do solemnly confess to the following. On the night of August 24, 1992, I took a kitchen knife from my drawer and stabbed my own daughter, Charlotte Manes, to death. I then deposited the body where it was later found. I did this alone, of my own accord and at the prompting of no other person.
>
> Sincerely,
> Mrs. George Benedict

I handed the paper to her. She sat silently and read what I had written.

"I took the knife from the island," she said almost absentmindedly. "It had been sitting there waiting for this moment, and the bitch didn't even look threatened. She lifted her dress past her belly and told me that my grandchild grew within it. So I drove that knife right into her guts. Once the blood flowed I felt wonderful. Turned the knife around and struck at her shoulder, then her neck. Her body turned as she fell and I knifed her again in the back. Finally I turned the body over and slit her throat."

She rose here and walked toward the desk where the pen lay.

"It felt perfect. It's what she came for. She knew what was coming. The surprised look on her face seemed false."

It was at this point that she crossed out the word *drawer* and put *island* above it. She did it neatly, and with a slight flourish, signed her name below. Then she handed it to me in the same way she had offered me my scotch—at full arm's length.

"There," she said. "It's finished. Now get out."

I took the signed confession and left.

The next day, in the evening papers, I read that Mrs. G. Benedict of Ridgefield, Connecticut, had died in her sleep, apparently from an excess of alcohol and barbiturates.

XXXVIII

JUST THE OTHER DAY I was crossing Seventh Avenue, a thoroughfare so decidedly one-way that God Himself would not risk venturing in the other direction. Teenagers, however, are another matter. Like spawning salmon, they find it impossible to do things the easy way, or, as opposed to my own obsessions, they are not much concerned with purity.

Certainly not the purity of one-way streets.

At any rate, I was trying to cross this river of rippling steel with the potentially terminal assumption that because it was a one-way street I needn't look in both directions.

"Hey! Hey, hey, hey!" I heard.

The voice contained a really annoying tone of infantile righteousness. I turned barely in time to see two bikes hurtling down upon me from the wrong direction. Seated atop them were two African-American adolescents.

"Hey! Hey, hey, hey!"

Now I, despite my preference for the hidden and the mysterious, am prone in these circumstances to experience the obvious: Fear. Images of my body being driven ruthlessly into the bumper of an oncoming car. Or, at best, being ridden over by these young rascals. Then there arrives the moment of righteous anger, muted by the still present sensation of having almost lost my life. Those were all fairly predictable.

However, I was quite unprepared for the very disturbing fantasy that followed. After I mumbled helplessly: "You're going in the wrong direction."

After that, I envisioned the following. That just as those two boys passed, I pushed both of them off of their bikes. It would not have been hard since they were forced to slow precariously for fear of also being driven into the oncoming traffic. After picturing them sprawled on the pavement, I imagined myself leaping quite uninhibitedly into the air and coming down, with all the force of my two extending feet, onto the head of the nearest offender. The skull appeared in my fantasy to crack open like a melon and the contents to go splushin' and sqwushin' all over that street. Brains bouncing wet and rubbery beneath the wheels of passing cars and trucks.

The unfortunate young man's companion would now be on his feet, eyes wide with amazement at the sudden demise of his friend. And then I saw myself, quite calmly, look the boy in the eye and say: "Young man, it is unfortunate that your friend could not honor the integrity of a one-way street."

At that point in the daydream, however, I looked down at my feet and saw jackboots. My legs were swathed in black jodhpurs. A riding crop dangled from my hand. My ordinarily friendly speech rhythms had changed to a kind of Viennese falsetto. Not unlike the Captain's exclamations in the Berg opera *Wozzeck*.

"WOZZECK, ER IST EIN GUTER MENSCH."

Now, the most surprising revelation this scenario inspired in me was the absolute conviction that no part of my vengeance fantasy was racially motivated. No. I am certain that had the Duke and Duchess of Windsor, or even General and Mrs. Robert E. Lee, been behaving with similarly carefree indifference toward my life, on some bicycle-built-for-two, I would have fantasized the exact same execution.

So, why did I find myself enrobed, head to foot, in an S.S. uniform?

Purity.

Ideological purity.

A one-way street is a one-way street! In that moment of Nazi transfiguration it appeared to me that Man, Woman, Civilization, Life, God Himself were centered in the ability of each individual to determine which direction a one-way street was headed.

Wasn't I just angry?

No. Had I been angry I would have pursued those rapscallions with my voice. I would still be yelling at them. For that brief moment of infernal imagery I was in the throes of hatred. What drove those two young men up that one-way street and almost into my lap may well have been anger. At me. At that very white part of Man-

221

hattan. However, in my case, my anger had been hoisted upon the wings of another, much darker construct. For that brief moment of diabolical fantasy, I was in the throes of hatred.

Fruit
of the pursuit
of purity.

Oh, I eventually returned to my sanity but not before reminding myself that every perfection I knew, every rule that I ever held sacred—all had been broken by God, every one of 'em. So when I hear mere mortals like myself, citizens of the United States, stand up and, in paragraphs they have given days of due consideration to, trot out phrases "un-American," or "moral war," or any other such inferences of purity and paradigm, I recall my own moments of such raving stupidity. But when these very ungentle folk—*of all races*, mind you—offer no apologies, and pursue these obsessions as if their insanity were salvation, I begin to hear the noise and feel the heat of ovens. I see the skull and crossbones of a much profounder disease than even racism. These people are in the pursuit of purity. And whatever form it takes, whether of morality or economics, social norms or race, or even one-way streets, the resolution is always the same—to crush the heads of the impure with the most unflinchingly righteous indignation. Even the citizens of Nazi Germany knew that race was petty. But in the pursuit of purity they felt pride.

As for goin' up one-way streets in the wrong direction, if Man *were* meant to honor them unswervingly, then Wilbur and Orville Wright would never have braved the winds of Kitty Hawk. James Joyce could not have reinvented Ulysses. And this entire nation would never have been created nor maintained. For you know and I know just from lookin' deep within ourselves that there is no more perversely tenacious one-way highway than our own resistance to the notion that all men are created equal.